# ABOVE *the*
# WATERFALL

## RON RASH

CANONGATE

This paperback edition published in 2017 by Canongate Books

First published in Great Britain in 2016 by Canongate Books Ltd,
14 High Street, Edinburgh EH1 1TE

www.canongate.co.uk

1

First published in the United States in 2015 by Ecco, an imprint of
HarperCollins Publishers, 195 Broadway, New York, NY 10007

*British Library Cataloguing-in-Publication Data*
A catalogue record for this book is available on
request from the British Library

ISBN 978 1 78211 801 5

Designed by Suet Yee Chong

Printed and bound in Great Britain by Clays Ltd, St Ives plc

MIX
Paper from
responsible sources
FSC
www.fsc.org   FSC® C018072

*For Philip Moore*

# ABOVE *the* WATERFALL

# PART ONE

*The moon an ungripped scythe*

Though sunlight tinges the mountains, black leather-winged bodies swing low. First fireflies blink languidly. Beyond this meadow, cicadas rev and slow like sewing machines. All else ready for night except night itself. I watch last light lift off level land. Ground shadows seep and thicken. Circling trees form banks. The meadow itself becomes a pond filling, on its surface dozens of black-eyed susans.

I sit on ground cooling, soon dew-damp. Near me a moldboard plow long left. Honeysuckle vines twine green cords, white flowers attached like Christmas lights. I touch a handle slick from wrist shifts and sweaty grips. Memory of my grandfather's hands, calluses round and smooth as worn coins. One morning I'd watched him cross the field, the steel oar rippling soil. In its wake, a caught wave of *sillion shine*. But this plow has wearied into sleep. How long lying here? Perhaps a decade, since saplings and saw briar rise amid broom sedge. Above all else, those bold yellow blossoms in full-petaled bloom. What has brought me here.

A deer emerges from the woods, nose up, stilt step then steadying pause, another hoof lifted. Dark rises around me. The black-eyed susans float like water lilies. All else disappears but they hold their yellow glow. Moon mirrors, sun ghosts. Dream abeyant. When the night-pond floods its banks, I walk the trail to the state park truck. Maybe another time, Les had answered when I invited him, claiming sheriff business to attend to. The trail steepens. When I look back at the meadow, only darkness.

*Lascaux.* What wonder to have made such a descent. Tar-pitched torch wood swabbing stone with light. Swerves and drops and slant downs. Dark rushing up behind each step. Then to find them there in the cave's hollow core—bison and ibex, but others lost elsewhere to the world: saber cats and woolly mammoths, irish elk. All live-motioned in the wavering light, girthed by curves of stone. Amid it all the runic human handprint. Where less art's veil between us and the world? How strange that Hopkins' quill scratches let me see more. *In*visioning before seeing. But the first message there inside the cave walls. What wonder yet echoes from the world's understory.

# One

_____

Where does any story really begin? One thing can't happen unless other things happened earlier. I could say this story began with an art class I took in ninth grade, or broken promises, one by Becky Shytle and one by me, or that it began when a shirtsleeve got caught by a hay baler's tines. Instead, I'll say it began on the Monday I first saw the blue cell phone, the same phone I held, briefly, in my hand the following Friday.

This all happened three weeks before I retired as county sheriff. There would be a meth bust on Tuesday, but otherwise I figured it to be an easy week—tie up some more loose ends, do a few more final favors, get my retirement paperwork done. I'd already quit coming in before midmorning, letting Jarvis Crowe, my replacement, get used to running things on his own. An easy week, but when I got to the office on Monday, Ruby, our day-shift dispatcher, let me know it would be otherwise.

"C.J. Gant called a few minutes ago, Sheriff. He's coming to see you. It's important, he said. Of course we know it's *always* important if it involves him or that resort."

"We do," I agreed. "Where are Jarvis and Barry?"

"Jarvis is checking out a break-in and Barry's serving a bench warrant."

"Anything else?"

"Not any crime," Ruby said. "Bobbi Moffitt was being her usual nosy self over at the café this morning. Said to me it didn't seem right for a man to retire at fifty-one. I told her thirty years for a lawman was like aging forty years for regular folks. And it is."

"I suppose so," I said. "I'm closing my door so I can try to figure out how to download these damn retirement forms."

"My grandson can come over and help you."

"I'll figure it out. I'd like to retire without some sixteen-year-old making me feel like an idiot."

"What about C.J. Gant?"

"Send him on in when he gets here."

The red light flickered on my office phone. The message was from Pat Newton, who owned the paper mill outside town. He'd offered me a part-time night watchman job, two twelve-hour shifts, one on Saturday and one on Sunday, starting next month. "I need an answer by next week, Les," Pat's voice said.

Clearing out my office. That was something else I needed to do, though that would be mainly filling trash cans, shredding old files. All I'd take with me would be some books off the shelf, a few things stashed in my desk. And the three paintings on the wall, two framed watercolors I'd done, each with a ribbon proclaiming BEST IN COUNTY, and the print of Edward Hopper's *Freight Car at Truro*.

*Even Hopper's boxcars are alone.*

That was the first thing Becky had said when she'd entered my office two years ago. Not how most people would start a conversation, but as soon as Becky said it I saw it too—the freight car hitched to no other. Not a single shadow other than its own. The sky empty.

*Yes, it seems so*, I'd answered that morning, our first exchange like passwords in a Masonic ritual.

I checked my e-mails from Becky, the first from last night.

*I wish you could have seen the black-eyed susans Friday night. They were transcendent, Les. Maybe another time you can go. There's something else, but it's not good. Darby took Gerald's lawn mower two weeks ago and still hasn't returned it. Can you help get it back?*

*I'll go see Darby this afternoon,* I typed, *but it's Gerald's fault letting Darby take it in the first place.*

Becky wouldn't see it that way, though. In her eyes Gerald could do no wrong, even though I'd cautioned her that Gerald wasn't quite the lovable old man that she thought.

Becky's second e-mail was from 9:06 today.

*There was a school shooting in Atlanta this morning.*

*Anywhere a school shooting happens, not just around here, I want to take extra precautions at the park.* Becky had told me that during her first office visit. By then I'd heard the scuttlebutt around town that Locust Creek Park's new superintendent was a *bit quair,* as the older folks put it—that she didn't own her own vehicle, just a bike, and no TV or phone. Not easy to talk to either, people said, some claiming Becky was autistic. *I'm not autistic,* she'd told me later, *I just spent a lot of my life trying to be.* New on the job, so overzealous, I'd thought at first. Then Becky had brought up an elementary school shooting in Emory, Virginia, in 1984. Two students and a teacher had been killed. She'd given enough details that I'd asked if someone she knew had been there. *I was there,* Becky had answered. I'd been curious enough afterward to Google *Becky Shytle,* but instead of something about the shooting, I'd found a news-paper photo of her and Richard Pelfrey, a terrorist who, had his timer worked right, would have killed more people than Ted Kaczynski and Eric Rudolph combined.

Two years and I still didn't know what word to use for our relationship. A few "dates," a few kisses. But more than anything, a wary out-of-step dance. Except for the first time I'd been in Becky's cabin. On that evening it had almost become more. I'd brought a bottle of wine and as Becky got us glasses, I'd sat on the couch and surveyed the cabin's front room, curious to see what it might reveal about her. There was a shelf of books, most connected to nature, but also some poetry and art books, including one I'd borrowed about the cave art in Lascaux. On the fire-board was a crumbling hornet's nest, a gold pocket watch, and a single photograph. In one corner a butter churn, in another corner a chair, a table, and a lamp. Except for the couch, that was it—no TV or CD player, no clock or radio or computer, no rug. Nothing on the walls, not even a cal-endar. The photograph of two old people, sun streaked and in an oval frame, seemed, like the rest of the room's con-tents, remnants left in a house long abandoned.

That night, for the first time, our kisses were the kind that led to a bed. But our talk was even more intimate, as if the room's feeling of time turned back allowed us to speak more freely of our pasts. Becky talked about her months with Richard Pelfrey, and I'd told her about my ex-wife Sarah, sharing things I'd never told anyone. Becky had also talked about her childhood, the shooting at her elementary school and what had happened in the months afterward. We spoke of promises.

But with the late hour and empty wine bottle came the feeling that we'd revealed too much, violated something within ourselves, the very thing that had attracted us to each other in the first place. So we had left it there for six months. More than once I'd imagined a listing on an Internet dating site:

Man who encouraged clinically depressed wife to kill herself seeks woman, traumatized by school shooting, who later lived with ecoterrorist bomber.

*Sorry to hear about the school shooting*, I typed, then remembered I needed to collect my monthly "stipend" from Jink Hampton. *I may be out and about later today. Will try to come by the park. Les*

Ruby once asked what sort of relationship Becky and I had. I'd answered that I didn't know the word for it, but a word came to me now.

*Accomplices*. Maybe that was what we were.

# *Two*

---

*Somewhere in Arizona a jaguar roams.* On this day of another school shooting, such news is so needed. Scat and paw prints confirm the sighting. Gone forever from the United States since the 1940s, many had believed. What more wonder might yet be: ivorybill, bachman's warbler, even the parakeet once here in these mountains. When I see them in dreams, they are not extinct, just asleep, and I believe if I rouse them from their slumber, we will all awake in the world together.

A fisherman is in the meadow, each backcast and cast a bowstring pulled and released. I walk upstream to check his license. As always, my chest tightens, so hard just to speak, especially the day of a shooting.

"The streams are about as low as I've seen them in a

while," the fisherman says when I hand the license back. "I was thinking that I might play golf this morning, and I probably should have. I've only had one strike."

He cradles the fly rod in the crook of his arm. I'm about to head back but he points upstream beyond the meadow and the road that leads past Locust Creek Resort to Gerald's farmhouse.

"I bet I'd get plenty of strikes over there," the fisherman says. "I heard they've stocked so many trout those fish line up like they're getting served at a cafeteria. You can throw in a bare hook and the trout will hit it. Anyway . . ." The man pauses and I raise my eyes. He's frowning now. "Pardon me for holding you up, Ranger. I was just trying to be sociable."

"I . . . I'm sorry," I stammer. "You aren't holding me up."

He nods and wades on upstream. It's almost noon so I return to the park office. I eat lunch at my desk, then pedal out to the Parkway. Bright-colored car tags pass like flash-cards. Land levels and I ride slow, a clock-winding pedal and pause. A pickup from Virginia sweeps past, leads me back thirty years to my grandparents' farm. There, old license plates were a scarecrow's loud jewelry. Wind set the tin clinking and clanking. But the straw-stuffed flour-sack face stayed silent. Those first months after my parents gave up and sent me to the farm, I'd sometimes stand beside the scarecrow, hoe handle balanced behind my neck, arms draped over. Both of us watchful and silent as the passing days raised a green curtain around us. Soon all we could see was the sky, that and tall barn planks the color of rain.

I had not spoken since the morning of the shooting. Then one day in July my grandparents' neighbor nodded at the ridge gap and said *watershed*. I'd followed the creek upstream, thinking wood and tin over a spring, found instead a granite rock face shedding water. I'd touched the wet slow slide, touched the word itself, like the girl named Helen that Ms. Abernathy told us about, whose first word gushed from a well pump. I'd closed my eyes and felt the stone tears. That evening, my grandfather had filled my glass with milk and handed it to me. *Thank you*, I said. A shared smile between them, from my grandmother's eyes a few tears. After that, more words each day, then whole sentences, enough to reenter school in September, though I'd stayed on the farm until Christmas.

The Parkway ascends, soon peers over landfall. No one is at the pull-off so I stop. Mountains accordion into Tennessee. Beyond the second ripple, a meadow where I'd camped in June. Just a sleeping bag, no tent. Above me that night tiny lights brightened and dimmed, brightened and dimmed. *Photinus carolinus*. Fireflies synchronized to make a single meadow-wide flash, then all dark between. Like being inside the earth's pulsing heart. I'd slowed my blood-beat to that rhythm. So much *in* the world that night. The next morning as I'd hiked out, I started to step over a log but my foot jerked back. When I looked on the other side, a copperhead lay coiled. Part of me not sight knew it was there. The atavistic like flint rock sparked. Amazon tribes see Venus in daylight. My grandfather needed no watch to tell time. What more might we recover if open to it? Perhaps even God.

I leave my bike at the pull-off. As I enter the woods, the wide, clean smell of balsam firs. Deeper, the odor of shadow-steeped mold. In canopy gaps, the sky through straws of sunlight sips damp leaf meal dry. For a minute, no sound. I gather in the silence, place it inside me for the afternoon. I coast back down the Parkway, the upward buffeting what a kite must feel. I pass a wheat field, its tall gold-gleaming a *hurrahing in harvest*. Soon Gerald and I will sit on his porch, a tin pan tapping as snapped beans fall. *You got no more family than me*, Gerald said when he learned my parents were dead and that I had no siblings. He'd told me about his son and his wife and his sister, all younger than him but now gone. I'm tired of being left behind, he'd said one day, eyes misting.

*But will be left never by me. Never by me. Never.*

# *Three*

C.J. Gant's daddy had been a decent farmer but bad to drink. He'd show up in town with fifty dollars in his pocket and wake the next day without a nickel. During elementary school, C.J. and his sister wore clothes that would shame a hobo, then had to hand the cashier a ticket to get the welfare lunch. In fourth grade, though, C.J. quit eating the cafeteria's meal, instead bringing lunches that were nothing more than a slab of fatback in a biscuit. He'd set the brown paper sack in front of him, trying to hide what he ate. Taunts about his father, shoves and trips, books knocked out of his hands, he'd had a full portion of misery. I'd never joined in the bullying, but I'd never done much to stop it either. C.J. never swung a fist or said a word back. Things got better in his teen years.

He and I both made extra money helping on his great-uncle's farm. The day C.J. turned sixteen, he began working afternoons and weekends at Harold Tucker's resort. He could buy himself clothes that didn't need patches, school lunches he didn't need a ticket for. He made good grades and received some scholarship money for college. He took out student loans, then worked two, sometimes three, part-time jobs to cover the rest.

You needed to remember all that when you dealt with C.J., because he rubbed a lot of people wrong, even those who knew his story. He took no small satisfaction in having a nice house in town and driving a pricey SUV. At public meetings he could come off as pompous, especially since he'd shed his mountain accent, but C.J. had done a lot of good since coming back five years ago—key fund-raiser for the downtown park and new high school, cosponsor of the county Meals on Wheels program. People could forget those things though.

C.J. had on his working duds, dark blue suit and white dress shirt with a silk tie. A golden name tag with TUCKER RESORTS PUBLIC RELATIONS was pinned on his coat pocket. When he sat down, C.J. laid his right hand on his knee, the way he always did, the East Carolina University class ring where you couldn't help noticing it.

"Come to bring me a retirement present?" I asked.

C.J. didn't smile.

"Gerald Blackwelder's poaching fish on resort property. You need to go see him, right now."

"Well, there's no need to get on your high horse about it, C.J. I'll warn him there's been a formal complaint."

"Warn him?" C.J. barked. "You by God drive out there and charge him. Our signs say we *prosecute* and they've been up six months. And if Gerald claims he wasn't up there, we've got the proof on camera."

"I think you know this county's got more serious problems than an old man poaching a few trout."

"He scared a guest enough that she left two days early. You think we can afford to lose customers, in this economy?"

"What'd he do?"

"He didn't have to *do* anything. Damn it, Les, he looks like he just walked off the set of *Deliverance*. Besides that, he's up there catching trout, and keeping them. How do you think our guests like that? They *pay* to fish and have to release their catch."

"I'm sure he just gets a few speckleds, not your pet rainbows and browns downstream."

"We've got guests who fish above the waterfall," C.J. said. "They appreciate how rare native brook trout are, and rarer still every time Gerald makes some his dinner."

"Brook" trout instead of "speckled," which was what C.J. had called them growing up. Something shed, same as his accent. I leaned back in my chair. C.J. and I had gotten crosswise before when he or Harold Tucker tried to tell me how to do my job.

"Why don't you just put it in your fancy brochures that Gerald's there to add to the rustic experience, an authentic mountain man fishing the old-timey way."

C.J. had always been good at keeping his feelings to himself, but now I could almost hear his molars grinding. But it wasn't just anger. He looked desperate.

"This isn't a joke, Les. I told Gerald in June not to go near that waterfall again. I put my ass on the line, instead of doing what Mr. Tucker wanted, which was to come to you. Gerald swore to my face he wouldn't go fishing up there anymore." C.J. grimaced and tapped the chair's arm with a closed hand. "If I'd thought it out, I'd have turned right to come see you instead of left to Gerald's house," he said, as much to himself as to me. Then C.J. leaned forward, his voice soft, "Les, if this isn't done right, I could lose my job."

He glanced down at his tie, then smoothed it with his hand, like the tie needed calming, not him.

"Come on, C.J.," I said, seriously, not joshing. "Don't you think you're overreacting a bit?"

"Have you seen our parking lot? If things don't pick up soon, Tucker will have to lay some people off."

"All right," I said. "I'll go this afternoon but I'm not charging Gerald without a warning."

"Damn it, aren't you listening?" C.J. said, raising his voice again. "He's *been* warned. By the signs, by me."

"But not by me," I said. "You can wait until after the end of the month and have Jarvis Crowe deal with this, but for now I'm still sheriff."

C.J.'s cell phone buzzed. As he took it from his pocket, I saw the puckered scar on the back of his hand, the result of a hay baler's metal tines on a long-ago Saturday morning. C.J.'s great-uncle had made a tourniquet from a handkerchief and we'd rushed C.J. to the hospital. *If your arm had gone in there it would have been ripped off and you'd have bled to death, son,* the doctor had told C.J., scolding him for his carelessness. But it hadn't been C.J. who'd been careless.

"You don't have to tell him anything," C.J. said to the caller. "I'm taking care of it right now. Just let me deal with it. I'll let Mr. Tucker know what's going on."

He pocketed the phone.

"I can't lose my job over this, Les," C.J. said. "My boys aren't going to grow up like me."

I'd thought to go to Jink Hampton's place first, but I raised my hands in surrender.

"Okay. I'll go on out there now and make it damn clear to Gerald that he will be arrested next time."

C.J. stood, but he didn't leave.

"You know this wouldn't have happened if Gerald

had sold that place two years ago. Even his nephew had the sense to know there'd never be a better offer. And now, with this recession, he'll be lucky to get half that."

"I'm sure you and Tucker had only Gerald's interests in mind."

"Think what you want," C.J. said, "but I knew that a man Gerald's age, especially one with a bad heart, would be better off with a hospital near."

"As far as I'm concerned, Darby inheriting less is all to the good. The only smart thing Gerald did was not to give that little prick of a nephew power of attorney. As for Gerald living longer, look what selling his farm did to your great-uncle. How long did he last in town, a month? You know what leaving a home place does to men like them. No hospital can cure that."

C.J. didn't have a response, because he knew it was true.

"Get over there, Les," he said, and left.

*You're smart, though you try to hide it. You can get away from this place too, be an art teacher in Charlotte or anywhere clear to Alaska.*

That's what C.J. had told me at the start of our senior year. Since he'd come back to live here, he'd never directly said anything about me staying put, though the first time he'd been in my office he'd nodded at the Hopper painting. "With the rusty wheels and those weeds, someone might see that painting as rather symbolic, Les. Is that why you bought it?" "I didn't buy it," I'd answered. "Mr. Neil gave it to me when he retired, frame and all. He just remembered that in class I'd liked Hopper's paintings."

I'd settled for too little in my life, C.J. believed. And maybe I had.

# *Four*

---

The school bus pulls into the lot and children stream from it into the world. They gather around the cedar announcement board, on it the brass plaque I placed there my first day.

> *HOW NEAR AT HAND IT WAS*
>
> *IF THEY HAD EYES TO SEE IT.*
>
> —G. M. *Hopkins*

I go through my usual protocol. No cameras or cell phones, not even for the teacher. Then we cross the bridge, go upstream where I show them cardinal flowers and bee balm, a mantis greenblended on a blackberry bush.

"It can change shades of color," I tell them and set the mantis on a dogwood limb. "If it stays, you will see."

I lead them to where joe-pye stems anchor low clouds of lavender.

"Did you know flowers grew so high?" I ask.

Solemn head shakes.

"I bet there is something else you don't know, that jaguars and parakeets once lived in these mountains. Most people think the parakeets have been gone for over a hundred years, but I know a man who says he saw some in 1944. I want to believe a few might still be around, don't you?"

The children nod.

I show them an empty hummingbird's nest, let them touch a box turtle's shell, other things. Last, we walk up above the bridge and sit on the stream bank. I point to a trout holding its place in the current.

"Let's try something," I say. "If you had a friend who'd never seen a fish swimming in a stream, what would you tell that friend the fish looks like? Think about that for a few minutes, without talking."

I watch and I too see something new, how the trout appears to weave the very water it is in. As if the world's first fish lay in dust, but with each fin and flesh thrum brought forth more water, soon whole rivers, then oceans. Taliesin in the coracle, the salmon of knowledge: all the world's wisdom waterborne, water born. Welsh notions Hopkins would have known.

"So what would you say to your friend?" I ask.

Several say a flag and the other children chime in.

"On a windy day."

"Not too windy."

"With lots and lots of rain."

"A brown flag with red spots."

"What if your friend asked how the fish was different from a flag?" I ask.

"No pole."

"It can't get dirty."

"Or be folded."

"Flags don't have eyes."

"Or mouths."

"Flags don't eat bugs."

The teacher nods at her watch, says it's time to leave. As the orange bus drives away, a child peers through the back window. Behind the glass she mouths words as she waves at me. Memory scalds. Not the orange-bright of buses we ran toward that morning but minutes before, in the classroom as Ms. Abernathy lined us up. *You must be as quiet as you can, children,* she had told us. *Promise me that you won't say a single word.* More memories come of the days and months after that morning: the room with big chairs and magazine-filled tables, a smaller room full of soft questions, a pair of black-framed glasses behind which huge eyes urged spoken answers, not head shakes. One night, my father thinking me asleep: *The other children are getting over it fine, why can't she? We've tried everything and it's cost us a fortune. What your parents offered, well, let them have her. At least we'll have a break from all this.*

I close my eyes. Wash away, I whisper. Wash away, wash away. I walk down the loop trail, pass foxglove past bloom. Midsummer their flowers dangled like soft yellow bells. I'd wished them a breeze so they might silently ring. The same yellow as Van Gogh's sunflowers. Vincent's thick paint, like Hopkins' thick sounds. Such grace-giving from supposed failed priests. I think of reading Hopkins in those days after Richard was killed. *A failed priest saved my soul.*

What would he see if here? I ask. I pick up a Fraser fir cone. A hollowed lightness like a thimble, spring's green weight gone. The edges are strong-keeled as viper scales, wing seeds wedged in the slits. High in a white oak, a flicker searches for grubs. The bird's too blended to see at first but then the red nape reveals and tree bark softens into feathers. The flicker's tap-bursts and pauses: a thoughtful message typed. Where the trail skirts the creek, a stand of silver birch, then a gap where sun and water pool. On a granite outcrop, a five-lined skink. *Plestiodon fasciatus.* Its throat fills and sags but no other movement, a chameleon of stillness. Indigo body coppered with stripes that chevron on the head. The back feet frog cocked, the tail a bright blue fuse. I too feel the heatsoak of sun and stone, the human in me unshackling.

# *Five*

One night the Discovery Channel showed a documentary about sheep in Wales. If the owner sold his flock, he had to sell the pasture as well, because, after so many generations, the sheep would be too rooted in that place to survive elsewhere. Little different for men like Gerald, I thought as I turned off the main road and onto the Blue Ridge Parkway. I'd seen others besides C.J.'s great-uncle leave houses where they and their families had lived for generations. They'd enter nursing homes or move in with sons or daughters. Like I'd told C.J., you'd be going to their funerals within six months.

I turned off the Parkway and passed the sign that said ENTRANCE LOCUST CREEK STATE PARK. I slowed and saw Becky's green state truck in the parking lot. I didn't turn in but followed the main road, soon passing another sign, LOCUST CREEK RESORT. On the left, the woods fell away, replaced by grass as manicured as a golf green, farther back the stone lodge itself. With its sixty rooms and three stories, the building parted the woods like a battleship, the same gray color and every bit as solid. A crazy idea, people had thought, turning the Tucker family's best bottomland into a tourist destination, but Harold Tucker had known what he was doing. He was a rich man now, with a second resort in Myrtle Beach. After college, C.J. had worked twelve years with an ad agency in Wilmington, but when a public relations position opened at Tucker's Myrtle Beach resort, he applied and got hired. Even after almost two decades, Harold Tucker had remembered him, and how hard C.J. worked for him as a teenager. The man believed in loyalty, and C.J. had been loyal to Tucker as well, which was why I figured he'd stick by C.J., even in a bad economy.

Where Locust Creek ran closest to the resort, a fly-fishing instructor stood beside a client dressed as if posing for an Orvis catalog, wicker creel and all. Not that he'd need much instruction. Tucker had the stream so well-stocked that all the guy had to do was hit water. Along the road's edge, spaced just yards apart, bright yellow signs:

*NO TRESPASSING*

*ALL VIOLATORS PROSECUTED*

I bumped over the culvert where Locust Creek entered a meadow on the state park side. Blacktop ended and gravel clattered as I crossed onto Gerald's property. He owned no cattle now, but the pasture's barbed wire fences didn't sag or the locust posts lean. A tin shed protected a Ford Red Belly tractor that a collector would pay good money for. I knew if I checked the oil stick, it would mark the right level and the fuel filter would be clean as a new sponge. Men of Gerald's generation took pride in such things, which made the patch of land beyond the woodshed appear so out of place. Charred wood and rusty tin poked out of kudzu and honeysuckle. It was all that remained of the house Gerald had built for his son, William.

Gerald was worming his tomatoes. He wiped his hands on his overalls and came to meet me. Even at seventy-six, he was a man not to be trifled with. Six feet tall and easily two-thirty, with little of that weight hanging over his belt. Gerald sheared his white hair and beard with scissors, keeping both short but ragged. Years back, a snapped logging chain had ripped open the right side of his face. The purple scar that stretched from eye to chin looked like a centipede had burrowed under his skin.

The scar and the size of the man, even the desert camo cap William had worn in Kuwait, all these things would have unsettled Tucker's guest. The story of your life is in your face, an old country song claimed, a hard life in

Gerald's case. How could it not be for a man whose only child died at nineteen. Now his wife, Agnes, was gone too. Over the years, he and I had gotten along well enough, but his anger could flare up like a struck match. When it did, people gave Gerald a wide berth. Yet you never saw that part of him when he was around Becky. Watching him dote on her, and her him, you'd think him the mildest of men. He looked that way now, smiling as we shook hands.

"Nice tomatoes," I said.

"They ought to be. Becky's got me fussing over them enough. But she's near convinced me she's right. I didn't dust a bit of Sevin on them. And feature how dark that corn is. I done it without pesticides too."

I looked at the field. The shucks had the right coloration, the tassels blond and silky.

Gerald tapped his chest.

"What with this bad ticker, I can't handle but an acre. Doc Washburn got on me for doing that much. Anyway, those tomatoes are riped up good so carry a few home with you."

"Thanks, but not today."

"So what brings you out this way, Sheriff?"

"Becky said that Darby's had your lawn mower for two weeks."

Gerald's smile disappeared.

"What of it?"

"I'm of a mind it's past time for him to bring it back."

Gerald looked down and scuffed up a bit of dirt with his boot toe.

"If that's why you come out here, I got nothing to say to you."

"Actually, it's not, Gerald. You scared a woman at the resort yesterday, bad enough that she packed up and left."

"I didn't mean to spook that woman," Gerald said. "The trail took a curve and of a sudden she was there. Hell, she give me a jolt too."

"C.J. Gant warned you not to go up there. Tucker's signs told you the same thing."

Gerald's chin lifted and his gray eyes narrowed.

"What about all the times Harold Tucker's bird watchers and flower sniffers come onto my land? I never rough-talked a one of them."

"That may be, but I'm here to tell you the next time you trespass I'll charge you."

"So you're taking their side?"

"The only side I'm taking is the law's. There are other places to fish. Go over to the park and catch your trout there. Becky's always glad to see you."

"Who claimed me to be fishing?" Gerald bristled. "Any that says so is a liar."

"Then why were you up there?"

As soon as I said it that way, I knew I'd made a mistake. Gerald's face, his whole body, grew taut.

"I'm not trying to pry into your business, Gerald," I said. "I'm just wanting to smooth this out, for everyone. C.J. Gant could get in trouble over this. He tried to do you a favor by not reporting you in June."

For a few moments Gerald didn't speak.

"I like to go up above that waterfall and look at them specks," Gerald finally said. "That water's so clear you can see every dot on them. It ain't about nothing but setting on a rock and watching them."

"That's good to hear," I said. "I'm glad you weren't poaching, but I'm afraid that still doesn't change anything. Tucker wants you to stay off his property and that's his right."

Gerald's fingers began rubbing his palms. He'd spent his life trying to figure out problems with his hands instead of with words, even so far as to build his son a house when William left for the Persian Gulf War. I'd always thought Gerald building the house was a sort of wordless prayer to ensure William's future—as if his son *had* to have a future if a house awaited him. But William hadn't come back. I'd been right behind the fire trucks the day Gerald had gotten the news about William. By then all that could be done was keep the fire from spreading. Gerald had been sitting on the ground, a charred door frame and empty kerosene can in front of him. Sparks had singed his shirt and arms but he didn't move or make a sound. No one could get him to, not even Agnes.

"This ain't right," Gerald said, his voice growing angrier. "I'm of a mind to go over there and tell Tucker my ownself it's not."

"You don't need to get put out about this, especially with your heart."

Gerald pointed at an overall pocket.

"I got my nitro right here if I have cause to need it."

"I'd rather those stay tucked in your pocket, Gerald," I said. "Look, I'll remind C.J. about resort guests wandering onto your property and I'll let him know you aren't catching their trout. I can talk to Tucker as well. This economy's got them on edge, same as a lot of folks. You can understand that. This will blow over if you'll just wait it out a bit. But I need you to promise you'll stay away from that creek, okay?"

That seemed to calm Gerald some. At least his fingers no longer rubbed his palms.

"Okay?" I asked again.

"Yeah," Gerald said.

"Becky been out to see you today?"

"She come by for a minute," Gerald said, his voice still sullen. "Why? You told her about this?"

"Not yet."

"It ain't your business to tell her."

"I think she needs to know."

"She'll take my side," Gerald said stubbornly.

I nodded at his field.

"You've got plenty around here to keep you busy. You take care of that corn and let me deal with the resort."

# *Six*

---

There were two photos of Richard Pelfrey and Becky online. One dated July 11, 2010, was of them at a strip-mining protest that had turned violent. Amid fists and tear gas, Becky and Pelfrey faced off. Screaming at him to stop, she'd told me. But in the earlier photo, taken that April, Pelfrey's arm was around her waist. The way she looked up at him, you could tell Becky loved him. People change, she'd said about Pelfrey, but it bothered me that Becky hadn't seen any change until he threw a tear-gas canister. You'd think after Pelfrey she'd be less certain about people, but not in Gerald's case, and now he'd not only trespassed but also put a good man in a tight spot.

Becky smiled as she came up the trail to meet me, but,

as always, her cheeks and brow tightened, causing a squint, as if smiling was a bit painful. She'd turned forty-three in April and, in spite of the girlish ponytail, her solid gray hair might cause some to think her older. Her face had creases from all the years outdoors, but Becky's eyes were youthful. They were blue, but a blue that darkened the deeper you looked into them. We gave each other our usual calibrated hug, neither casual nor intimate. The drab uniform couldn't hide Becky's narrow waist and firm breasts and hips. Just brushing against them brought memories of the night at her cabin.

"I'm sorry to hear about what happened in Atlanta," I told her as I stepped back. "I know it brings back bad memories."

Becky's shoulders hunched slightly, hands linked in front of her, as if even after three decades, just the mention of a school shooting caused her to make herself a smaller target. For a few moments the only sound was the stream. A kingfisher crossed low overhead and Becky watched it, though *watching* didn't seem the right word for how intently she followed the bird's flight. She did the same with a spider's web or a wildflower. The first time I'd seen her do it, I'd thought it an affectation. It wasn't though, it was a connection. The kingfisher followed the stream's curve and disappeared.

"Those flowers Friday night were like a Monet painting," Becky said, brightening, "except better because the flowers were alive."

"Sorry I missed that."

"I want to show you something," Becky said, and took my hand, leading me across the bridge.

"If this is another episode of *Nature's Wonders*, it needs to be a short one."

"It is," Becky said, and smiled.

We walked up to where the creek curved. The meadow appeared, behind it the road and across it Tucker's lodge.

"Here," Becky said, pointing at a blackberry bush.

But before I looked closer, I heard Gerald's truck, then saw it bump over the culvert where Locust Creek entered the park, dust rooster-tailing in its wake as Gerald turned into the resort's drive.

"I've got to go," I told Becky.

I walked fast and then trotted, the bridge's planks shuddering as I crossed. Becky followed, shouting for an explanation.

"Gerald's gone to the resort to cause trouble," I said and got in my car, already cursing myself, because I should have known this might happen.

When I got there, Gerald was facedown on the lodge's concrete sidewalk. A security guard jabbed a knee into Gerald's back, while his right hand held a Beretta's muzzle inches from Gerald's head. Another security guard stood beside them. Tucker shouted at the guard from the porch as I warned him to put the gun on the ground. Becky's truck door slammed and she ran toward us, shouting as well. The guard looked up at me but didn't put the pistol down until Tucker nodded. I picked it up and saw the safety was off.

Becky grabbed the guard by the collar and jerked so hard he tumbled off Gerald and onto his back. Sobbing, she helped Gerald to a sitting position. The right side of his face looked like a sander had been at it. Becky talked to him but Gerald was too dazed to understand. His pill bottle lay on the ground and Becky took out a nitroglycerin tablet and pressed it into his mouth.

"He okay?" I asked.

"His heart at least," Becky said. Tears still streamed down her face as she turned to the guard. "You had no right to do this. No right."

"He damn well did," Tucker shouted as he came down the porch steps. "He was doing his job, protecting me."

Instead of his usual suit and tie, Tucker wore a blue polo shirt and white khakis, probably planning on an afternoon of golf, at least before this happened. I raised an open palm and warned Tucker not to come nearer. I went over and set my free hand on Becky's shoulder. Her whole body shook, but the sobs had stopped.

"It's okay. Just take care of Gerald," I said, keeping my

hand on her shoulder as I turned to Tucker. "What in the hell happened?"

"He came up here cursing and raising hell," Tucker said, "saying he'd come to set things straight with me and nobody, including my guards, was going to stop him. I've got witnesses."

"Did he physically assault you?" I asked. "Did he threaten you directly?"

"I didn't give him the goddamn chance," Tucker bristled. "Why the hell do you think I have security?"

"Did Gerald have a weapon?" I asked the security guard.

"No, but he said he was going inside to see Mr. Tucker and that we couldn't stop him."

"So you shoved an old man onto concrete and pulled a gun on him?"

"They were doing their job, Sheriff," Tucker said.

Gerald muttered something to Becky.

"He wants to get up," she said to me.

Becky and I helped Gerald to his feet. He looked around but he seemed unable to focus. Becky placed a hand on his arm to steady him.

"Get him to the doctor," I told Becky.

She kept the hand on Gerald's arm as he shuffled to her truck.

"You're not taking him straight to jail?" Tucker asked

incredulously. He raised a hand to the hearing aid plugged into his right ear, as if it had surely malfunctioned. "Are you shitting me?"

With his heavily creased face, unconcealed hearing aid, and no attempt at a comb-over of what hair he had left, Tucker seemed reconciled to his age, until you noticed his body. He wasn't a tall man, five eight or so, but wide-shouldered, his body veeing to a narrow waist. Tucker had played football at NC State in the late sixties and even at seventy he radiated a running back's compact, barely contained power. It wasn't just golf that kept him in shape. I'd seen him at the Y in town, working with a trainer and always using free weights, not the machines. I felt that power directed at me now, and plenty of frustration.

"No," I answered. "If your people had handled this right, I might be. That Beretta your security guard pointed at Gerald had its safety off. If I'm arresting anyone, it's your employee for reckless endangerment."

"Is that right about the safety?" Tucker asked the security guard.

The guard began to mutter something in his own defense, but Tucker cut him off.

"Get out of my sight before I fire you," Tucker said, and turned to me. "I'm still swearing out a warrant on Gerald."

"Fine, but I'll not serve it."

Tucker wasn't a man used to people bucking him. He looked about to say something more, then abruptly turned and walked back up to the porch where C.J. now stood. Tucker passed him without any acknowledgment. I was about to speak to C.J. but he turned and went inside as well.

# *Seven*

The smell of a room soaked in long silences, dusty quilts and mothballs, linger of linseed oil and mildew. My grandparents' bedroom had been much the same, even the mattress sagged by weight and time. Those nights I came frightened but silent to their bed, a wordless shifting to make room. Worn springs soothingly sighed as feathers nestled around me. At breakfast come morning, no TV or radio or much said, allowing night's stillness to linger, never asking more of me than a head shake or nod. My grandfather's words when my parents brought me: *This girl will talk when she's ready.*

The ladder-back chair's legs scrape as I get up. Across the room, bedsprings stir but Gerald does not wake. I leave the house and walk to the barn. Grasshoppers launch, then land, the high stalks swaying. On a loud orange trumpet vine flower, a swallowtail's blue wings open and close in slow applause. Caught on an angelica tree, a black snake's cast-off stocking. Closer, ribs of milk traces, manure scabs the color of oatmeal.

The so-much of memory as I step into the dark and wait: always back then believing my grandparents' barn was asleep until I'd entered, light's slow emergence like one eyelid drowsily lifted. Even now something of that feeling as I step farther inside. In the corner the duster and pesticides I've talked Gerald out of using. Beside them a pitchfork and a kerosene can. A barn swallow flutters in the loft, then the parabolic swoop toward thicker light. On a stall door a leopard slug. *Slug*: its body a slimy slow lugging, and yet, the twice-pronged crown, the long robe's silver wake. The slow going forth magisterial, as I'd seen as a child, now see again.

Good memories that even now can heal. Those mornings when I laddered to the loft, made my straw manger beside the square bale door. There on the straw-strewn floor, a sundial of slanted light. I'd reach my child's palm into it, hold sunspill like rain. Eyes adjusting, much more revealed: junctions knit with spiderwebs, near cross beams dirt dauber nests, the orange tunnels rising like cathedral pipes. Sometimes a shadow suddenly fleshed, long black tail draining into the straw. The few sounds soothing, swallow wings rustling, insect hum. Then my grandmother's voice. *Come, child, it's time to eat.*

I step out into noon's startling whiteness. Gerald still sleeps so I sit on the porch and take out my notebook, read the entries I wrote last week.

> *the hummingbird nest at the meadow edge—a strawy*
> > *thimble*
> *the hummingbird's wings—stained glass alive in*
> > *sudden sunlight shimmer*
> *wildflowers sway in their florabundance*
> *the grasshopper's rasping papyrus wings*

I take out my pen, remembering what I felt when Les came and placed his hand firm on my shoulder.

> *even the hermit thrush calls out to the world*

# *Eight*

I was plenty put out with Gerald, but I'd told Becky I'd do it, so at five o'clock I left the office and drove to Darby Ramsey's house. The place was in no better shape than other times I'd been there, Darby's idea of home improvement hanging a satellite dish on a sagging gutter. He hadn't cut his grass in months and I didn't see Gerald's lawn mower. A woman who looked to be in her mid-thirties stood on the porch, a blue cell phone pressed to her ear. She wore jeans and an oversize orange-and-white football jersey that made her look even skinnier than she was. But the number 13 seemed right for any woman hanging around Darby. When I got closer, I saw more than time had aged her. Eyes sunk deep in their sockets, teeth nubbed and colored like Indian corn, scabby chin. A fine addition to a *Girls on Meth* pinup calendar.

Inside, a toilet flushed. I knew what that was about, but at least I'd cost the asshole some drugs. The front door opened and Darby came out wearing only jeans, tousling his hair like he'd just gotten up. He lit a cigarette and smiled. His teeth weren't wrecked like his lady friend's, but the loose jeans argued graduation to meth-head status since I'd last seen him. I couldn't help but think of William, Darby's first cousin, who was dead at nineteen while Darby was still alive. *Justice.* You'd think a lawman would have some faith in that word, but in thirty years I'd seen too little of it.

The woman said, "Got to go," and put the cell phone in her pocket.

"Come to ask me to be your replacement, Sheriff?" Darby asked.

Even halfway whittled to bone Darby still had a strut about him. I looked into eyes the color of dirty motor oil.

"No," I answered, "convicted felons can't be sheriff."

"Just the unconvicted ones, I guess," Darby said, and turned to the woman. "The sheriff here takes good care of the pot dealers around these parts, and they take care of him. Gives the sheriff more time to bother folks like me who ain't in on the deal."

I stepped past Darby and went into the front room. With no light and the blinds pulled down, it was hard to see much, but there was no cat-piss smell, so they weren't cooking.

"Where's your uncle's lawn mower?" I asked. "He needs it back."

"Uncle Gerald ain't said that to me," Darby said. "That hippy park ranger sent you out here, didn't she? I know what she's up to. That land's been death-bed promised to me and Gerald ain't changing that will because some bi—woman acts all concerned and caring about him."

"Becky does care about him, unlike you."

For a moment, I thought about telling Darby what had happened at the resort but decided not to. He'd find some way to turn it to his advantage.

"You don't know what I care about," Darby sneered.

"All I've got to do is look at you to know what you care about," I answered. "Another month and you'll need no more than a shoestring to keep those jeans up over your scraggly ass. What about that lawn mower?"

"If you see it, take it," Darby said, and motioned the woman inside the house. "You got any other business with me?"

"Not today," I said, and Darby followed the woman inside.

Twice I'd put Darby in jail for six months. The meth, however, could soon put him away for good, six feet deep. Even with a bad heart, Gerald might outlast him. A man entering his coffin. That was what came to mind when Darby followed the woman through the oblong door and into the dark. Darby shut the door, and I had a pleasing image of a wooden lid slowly closing over him. Smoke it, mainline it, whatever will do the job, just go ahead and do it.

Go *ahead and do it.* The same thought I'd had eleven years ago, but back then I had said it aloud.

# *Nine*

At the Sierra Club meeting, some left while Richard still spoke. Others fell silent, and made quick exits after he finished. A coal company bulldozer had shoved a thousand-pound boulder off a mountain and killed a child. After two years of delays by coal company lawyers, the state court ruled the company had been negligent. Punishment: a five-thousand-dollar fine. *Can't you people see this is a bare-knuckle fight,* Richard had told us. *A three-year-old is crushed to death and you talk about fund drives? You don't think it will happen again to another child?* After the meeting, I alone stayed. *Let me guess,* he'd said. *You work at a library or a bookstore. You want to save the world if it doesn't take more than one evening every two weeks. You love "nature" but never camped more than a quarter mile from asphalt.*

*I'm a park ranger, at Shenandoah,* I'd answered. *I camp where I see no humans for days. What happened to that child, I don't want that to happen again, ever.*

Four months together. I worked at the park while Richard, who was good with his hands, made money as a handyman and from the honey harvested from his bee hives. Most of our food came from his garden. On days and nights we had free, Richard and I camped in places where no one else went. We attended biweekly meetings where no one spoke of donations and land easements. Not quite Earth First! but close. Confrontation but not physical violence, we all agreed, including Richard, though the words *par tous les moyens nécessaires* were tattooed on his forearm. It was Richard who had planned a demonstration on the anniversary of the child's death. Not at the mine site but at the company's headquarters. *We may do some riverbank cleanup afterward,* Richard told me that morning, and handed me my steel-toed work boots. He hefted a backpack onto his shoulder as we were leaving. *Snacks and water,* he said.

Locals joined us that day, some whose tap water was slurried with coal, but most, like us, outraged by both the child's death and the verdict. In front of the office, two policemen and a company security officer stood on the sidewalk. Outside the yellow tape with us, two newspaper reporters, one with a camera draped around her neck.

Richard held no sign. He watched and waited, the back-pack in his hand. *Coiled*, I realized later.

"Child killer," a local woman shouted when a man in a suit came out of the building. She raised a jar filled with gray water. "And now you're going to kill the rest of us with this."

The man walked toward the parking lot, head down, until the woman threw the jar. Glass shattered and the water soaked his pants.

"Fucking bitch," he said.

The woman surged forward and the yellow tape snapped. Then she stepped back, as if the tape were dangerous, like a downed power line. No one else crossed, until Richard's tear-gas canister clanked on the concrete, spun once, and detonated. Then smoke and coughs and curses, thicker sounds of struck flesh. A hand slapped me and the taste of rusty iron filled my mouth. As the gray lessened, I saw Richard and, between us on the ground, the man in the suit. Richard swung his boot and a rib cracked, audible as a rifle shot. Richard kicked again and the steel toe drove the man's front teeth into his throat. Then a camera flashed and sirens wailed. A few moments later a policeman shoved me aside, kept his gun on Richard while another officer handcuffed him.

He got out on bail the next day. As I'd packed my last belongings, he'd offered me the newspaper photograph.

*You're looking at me, but who were you really angry at, Becky?*
Richard had said. *I think you might have started in on that
bastard yourself if we'd had another few seconds.*

I sit up in bed, unable to sleep. Too many echoes of
the past, Gerald on the ground, the guard's gun, the school
shooting. I try to follow the dream that sometimes leads
me into sleep: the iron ring that opens the concrete door,
then the descent into the low cave where the lost animals
wait. But tonight I can't grasp that ring. I pull on a T-shirt
and go out on the cabin's porch, try to turn my thoughts
to what I will show the schoolchildren tomorrow. But
memory nags. After my grandparents' deaths, I let no one
get close, not in college or grad school, twelve years at the
Shenandoah park.

Until Richard. When the FBI said he was responsible, I didn't believe them, despite what Richard had told me
two weeks earlier. This was an office with a dozen workers, not an empty vacation house. Even when the news
reported that part of his boot matched a pair worn at a
rally, I told myself it was coincidence. But then the jawbone
with four back teeth, two fillings a dental X-ray confirmed.
How could I have been so wrong about someone? Perhaps
my father was correct: I should have *gotten over it like the
other children.* If I had known more people, really known
them, learned from them . . .

A nighthawk is near, its call electric, brief: a cicada's

first syllable. Farther off a barred owl calls. Such sounds may soothe me into sleep, into the dream of where the iron ring yields to my grasp. But as I go back inside, I also take my grandfather's watch from the mantel, free the gold chain from its fob, and place the chain around my neck.

# PART TWO

# *Ten*

Trey Yarbrough opened his pawnshop at 9:00 A.M. except Fridays and weekends, so on Tuesday morning I had time to stop in after confirming with Jarvis that the raid was on. Trey sat on a stool behind the counter, a silver trumpet in one hand and a rag dabbed with polish in the other. The windowless cinder-block walls, coated thick with white paint, were bare and bright as an interrogation room. Which seemed a smart move on Trey's part. Plenty of his customers had bad memories of such rooms, as well as a desire to conduct business in places not so well lit, so were probably less likely to haggle.

On the shelf behind Trey, a twenty-gallon aquarium held a timber rattlesnake thick as a man's wrist. Wrapped behind its wedged head was a necklace of copper wire, attached to the wire a small ring. A message taped above the tank said THIS FELLOW IS LET OUT EVERY NIGHT. I CUT THE POWER TO THE LIGHTS BECAUSE HE LIKES CRAWLING AROUND IN THE DARK. BREAK IN IF YOU FEEL <u>REAL</u> LUCKY.

"Interested in a trumpet, Sheriff?" Trey asked. "One of your deputies could play the cavalry charge when you take on the bad guys, like in that *Apocalypse Now* movie."

"Taps would be more like it, since I've got less than three weeks left, though I wouldn't mind borrowing your snake to pitch inside a trailer later today. Keep us from having to go inside."

"Another meth bust?"

"Yeah."

Trey stepped back and tapped the aquarium, triggering a sound like a maraca. When the tail stilled, I counted nine buttons.

"Two months and not a scratch on my doorknobs and locks," Trey said. "No dead bolt or security system ever did that."

"You really let that thing out at night?"

"Damn straight. If they break in, it ain't about scaring. I *want* it to bite the sons of bitches. Of course they got more poison running through them than that snake does. It'd likely be the one worse off."

"Probably so."

Trey started polishing the trumpet again. He was at

least sixty but his curly gray hair reached his shoulders. On weekends, he played guitar at the Skinned Cat with some other old-school rock and rollers. Trey was good, gifted with long fingers whose nails he kept carefully manicured, but what you'd notice first about Trey was his eyes, one blue, the other gray. Guess my DNA hedged its bets during the Civil War, he liked to joke.

"So what you looking for?" Trey asked.

"Officially, a TV and a chain saw."

"Just the last few days?"

"Yeah," I said, "a break-in."

"No TV or chain saw, but damn near everything else. One fool came in with a hearing aid yesterday, said he'd pulled it out of his daddy's ear when the old man died that morning. I should have done the world a favor and shot the bastard. You ever think it would come to this? I swear to God, Les, it's got so bad I can't find the words to describe it, can you?"

"Job security," I said.

"I guess so, for the likes of us," Trey sighed. "But if you deal with our kind of clientele long enough, you start wondering why God just don't lick a finger and thumb and snuff out the whole damn thing. You're smart to go ahead and get out. So first of the month, you're officially retired?"

"First of the month."

"How's that cabin of yours coming along?"

"Good. It should be done by December."

"Billy Orr does good work," Trey said.

"He does, and he doesn't let you forget it when he hands you the bill."

"For sure," Trey said, and set the trumpet in the display case. "So what else are you looking for?"

"Did Darby Ramsey bring in a lawn mower?"

"Yeah, last week, but I sold it yesterday."

"It was Gerald's."

"He's one shameless piece of shit, ain't he?" Trey said. "I figured he hadn't come by it honest, but if I'd known it was Gerald's, I wouldn't have took it. He's a rough old coot but I like him."

"Well, let me know if Darby brings in anything else. I'd love to bust his ass one more time before I retire."

"If he shows up with something, I'll call you," Trey said. "Be safe today doing that meth bust. You're in the home stretch."

Outside, the sun had hauled itself completely over the mountains. It was going to be a warm day, which would make being in the hazmat suit all the more miserable. Mist Creek Valley, that was where we'd be going, though enough meth got cooked there that Jarvis had renamed it Meth Creek Valley. Rodney Greer looked to be one of those cookers, because last week before dawn Jarvis had hidden his patrol car on a logging road and walked up to

Greer's trailer, kicked up Sudafed foil packets among a trash heap's ashes.

Ruby was at her desk when I entered the office.

"Did the judge call?" I asked.

"No, was he supposed to?"

"Only if Harold Tucker asked for a warrant. How about around here? Anything I need to know about?"

"Jarvis was looking for you earlier but he stepped out," Ruby said. "Barry's downstairs double-checking the equipment. You know how he is about that."

"It's good to have someone that careful around," I said. "You make sure they're still doing it after I'm retired."

"You know I will," Ruby said. "But you be sure to look after my boys today."

*My boys.* That's what she called Jarvis and Barry. She especially doted on Barry, who was still in his twenties, just eight months on the job. Ruby had been here long enough to know anything from a traffic stop to a domestic could get an officer killed, but like the rest of us, she worried most about the meth raids. I knew that as soon as we left she'd take a St. Christopher medal from her desk and rub it while she prayed we would come back safe, a Southern Baptist calling for backup.

"Don't worry," I said. "I'll look after them."

"And yourself too," Ruby added.

I'd been in my office only a few minutes when Jarvis

knocked on the door. With his freckles and cowlicked red hair, hazel eyes that never seemed completely awake, Jarvis looked more like a teenager rousted out of bed than a man almost forty.

"I'll soon start getting my stuff out of here," I said as he sat down.

Jarvis blushed.

"I'm not wanting to rush you, Sheriff."

"I know that but you need to get settled in. As far as what's on the walls, I can leave the calendar, the state map too."

"Sure," Jarvis said, and pointed a finger at the water-color behind me. "I don't guess you'd be willing to sell that one, would you? I've always liked it. It's calming to look at it, which I expect I'll be needing a lot more of in a few weeks."

I looked back at the painting as well. Dark blue mountains rising into a light blue sky. In the lower-right corner, L.C. '94.

"I won't sell it, but I will leave it here for now."

"Thanks," Jarvis said. "You won't mind if I hang it on this side of the room, will you?"

"That's fine," I said, turning to face him. "So you're sure Greer's been cooking?"

"I'm sure," Jarvis said, "and not just because of what was in the trash pile. You know how these places are. It had that dead feel about it."

I did know. Some of it you could see, windows closed and shades pulled down, doors never opened wide. There might be a grill or horseshoe pitch out front but they never looked used. Everything appeared not so much left behind as surrendered in a siege. A white flag raised. *Just let us have the drugs and the rest is yours.*

"And Ben Lindsey's daughter is still with Greer?" I asked.

"I drove by there yesterday and her car was there."

"Any sign of diapers in that trash heap?"

"I didn't see any."

"Maybe she at least has enough sense left to leave the baby with her parents," I said. "She's done that before."

"I hope to God so," Jarvis said.

The worst thing was finding a child inside. You'd approach the house or trailer lots of time not knowing. Then you'd see a toy or baby food jar and get a knot in the belly. Things normally associated with happiness, like a teddy bear or pacifier, became ominous as headlights beaming up from a lake.

"But no other adults there, right?"

"Didn't look to be."

"Then I'll tell SBI to just be backup," I said. "Barry's downstairs getting out the Tyvek and respirators. You'd better go check on him. You know how he gets if he thinks a child might be involved."

"I know," Jarvis said.

Jarvis went downstairs. Because of his boyish looks, he might get tested early on, but he'd proved that he was plenty tough enough for the job. After Jarvis backed down the big talkers, busted a few heads if necessary, the word would get around. Tough but not sadistic. I couldn't see Jarvis beating a drifter senseless with a blackjack or strip-searching some kid just because he could. He'd make mistakes but he'd learn from them. Jarvis would do fine.

It was almost eleven. I always liked some coffee and a few minutes of downtime before a raid, but before heading over to Greene's Café, I Googled "Sarah Barker" and "Hoyt Counseling Center." An updated staff photograph appeared. The first thing I noticed was that the silver earrings looked new. Their design was triangular, perhaps a pyramid or a mountain. A gift from her husband or maybe one of her sons. Sarah's eyes were the same, green with flecks of gold-brown, and there was life in them. The sides of her mouth argued more smiles than frowns. I enlarged the photograph. Her hair was shorter, a bit more gray. Maybe another line on her brow, throat a bit looser. Looking for signs of aging, enough that one day I might be able to tell myself, *See, this is not the woman who came wading out of the river that afternoon, smiling and bare but for the water glistening off her.*

Sarah had a good life now, three kids, a husband, the Lexapro working. After her first child was born, she'd begun sending me Christmas cards. I'd watched her family grow, the photo more crowded with each new child, the steady rise in their heights. *Season's Greetings from the Barkers.* The first year I'd sent a Christmas card back, addressed to the whole family, but never after that. After five years the cards quit coming and I was glad. *To show you I'm all right and whatever you did or didn't do is forgiven* was one way to look at the cards. But a darker part of me couldn't help thinking Sarah was also saying *See what you might have had.* Evoking the broken promise of that long-ago afternoon on the river, when Sarah and I were happy and in love and vowing to stay so the rest of our lives.

I studied the photograph a few more moments and thought about yesterday how I'd felt sadness for Becky at the resort. But another part of me had felt vindicated. *See, Gerald's not what you thought he was. He can be filled with rage and violence.*

At the café, the breakfast patrons had left and the lunch crowd hadn't arrived, so I was the only customer. I took my usual seat in the back booth and Lloyd brought me my coffee.

"See any rain clouds out there, Sheriff?"

"Afraid not."

"If it gets any drier, the catfish will be carrying canteens."

"I reckon so."

"That going to bother you?" Lloyd asked, nodding toward the counter's radio.

I shook my head. Because they were busy preparing lunch on Sundays, Lloyd and his wife, Betty, listened on Tuesdays to a rebroadcast of the church service.

As I sipped my coffee, the congregation sang "Will There Be Any Stars in My Crown." The piano was the same one I'd grown up listening to, rickety and never quite tuned right, but the music felt all the more sincere because of it, the same with the congregation's mismatched singing. I recognized a couple of voices, older, a bit shakier, still fervent. At the hymn's conclusion, rustles and murmurs as the hymnals got stashed in the pew pockets. Preacher Waldrop began the opening prayer. He was over eighty but his voice remained strong and vigorous.

After the prayer, Preacher Waldrop read aloud from the book of Mark, the passage where Peter walks on water before getting scared and sinking. Then he launched into his sermon.

"There Peter was, with Christ Almighty standing right afore him, the fellow even now called the rock of the church, and Peter floundering away with no more grace than a three-legged mule. Ponder it. The same Peter that seen the lame trot off without a stumble, blind folks with their eyes awash in every color of the rainbow. Peter had been there to witness it all. His own eyes seen the dead wiggle out of grave quilts like a moth shucking its cocoon. Have you seen such a sight in your woods or fields, brothers and sisters? I have. It was of an afternoon and I thought that cocoon was nothing more than a fox turd. They ain't no way to say it but that. All brown and dried-up looking. Then that cocoon give a shiver and this little head poked through and then its body spread out as pretty a set of wings as I've seen on bird or butterfly. Big green wings, the very color of new life itself. Now you're thinking, Preacher, you was talking about old Peter and now you're talking about moths. Brothers and sisters, it's all one. There Peter was, looking straight into the very eyes of God, walking the Sea of Galilee and then of a sudden up to his neck in water. Some would argue he lacked the true believing, but I say he had enough faith to go it a ways, and when he couldn't go farther Christ fetched him up. What am I saying? I'm saying that the walk to God ain't easy for the best of us. Now some would say, Preacher, if Peter had misdoubts there in the very glory of the Lord, what of us left here that ain't seen the dead raised nor the leper folk healed. All we seen is hard trials and sorrows. I'd not deny it. Burdens are plenty in this world and they can pull us down in the lamentation. But the good Lord knows we need to see at least the hem of the robe of glory, and we do. Ponder a pretty sunset or the dogwoods all ablossom. Every time you see such it's the hem of the robe of glory. Brothers and sisters, how do you expect to see what you don't seek? Some claim heaven has streets of gold and all such things, but I hold a different notion. When we're there, we'll say to the angels, why, a lot of heaven's glory was in the place we come from. And you know what them angels will say? They'll say yes, pilgrim, and how often did you notice? What did you seek?"

I could almost hear Becky offer a soft amen as Lloyd turned down the radio and came over with his coffeepot.

"He can still whittle out a bully sermon, can't he?"

"It seems so," I said.

"And a good man too. I've never heard a bad word told against him."

I nodded, because it was true. He was a good man. On that evening eleven years ago, Preacher Waldrop had come to the hospital and sat with me an hour while we waited to see if Sarah would live. He could tell I didn't want to talk about it and he respected that. When the doctor gave us the word, Preacher Waldrop touched my shoulder and left.

I paid Lloyd and walked back across the street. You can see heaven all around us, Preacher Waldrop claimed. But Mist Creek Valley would soon confirm that the same was true of hell.

# *Eleven*

---

*Chkkk chkkk.* A red-winged blackbird saying *away from me keep, away from me keep* as he commandeers a cattail masthead, ebony coat blazoned with red epaulets fringed white. Above the drainage pond, galax's skunky scent. Nearer the stream, cardinal flowers bloom. I touch a petal, some moisture yet. I check the campsites, then head back to the bridge. I set both arms on the railing, look down. Always a dizzying raft feel first, wood and water both moving, then only water as the bridge staples to the banks. Months past their name, mayflies emerge. *Ephemeroptera.* Brief lives spent aloft, they drift down light as dandelion spores. A brown trout sips one off the surface. Beneath the trout, mica-flecked sand gleams white. Come fall the female's caudal fin will nudge the grains to make a nest, her eggs spilling like pearls into a purse.

The trout rises and curves. On its flank the spots Hopkins calls *rose moles*. A water snake, bankblended until now, unspools into the water, prow headed as it swims across, rests in the opposite shallows. On its back, inscape of dark brown saddle marks with thin pyramids of yellow. Last week a man had brought one to the office, two children in tow. Killed a moccasin, he bragged. I'd shown the children how a viper's head differed, explained why all snakes were needed, including the venomous ones. This snake swivels downstream, a current within a current, soon under the bridge. As I turn to watch it reemerge, Carlos comes up the trail, a child's plastic bucket in his hand.

"Look at this, Beck. A kid caught it above the beaver ponds." Carlos holds the bucket between us. "I thought it was a brook trout fingerling at first."

A yellow-orange belly, dark flank dotted, but not a trout.

"*Percina aurantiaca*," I tell Carlos. "The common name is tangerine darter or river slick."

"I've never seen one before," he says. "What's their range?"

"The Tennessee River and its tribs."

"Endangered?"

"A few more dams and they will be."

"I can put it in a bigger bucket if you want to show the kids in the morning."

"No," I say. "Release it."

"Okay," Carlos says, glances at his watch. "Do you mind taking your break first?"

I nod and go to the truck and get my notebook, cross the bridge, and enter a stand of hardwoods. Crackle of leaf meal, roll of acorn under my boot. Even in drought these woods damp smelling. I sit with my back against a tulip poplar. But before I take out my notebook and pen, a glimpse of orange and yellow between trees. I walk to the wood's edge. Near the meadow, two orioles perch on a sycamore limb. Always the hope that somehow my dreams of the cave animals might be a summoning. *What he claimed to see*, an ornithologist had once told me, noting that the last wild Carolina parakeet had been collected in 1904. But Gerald had the colors right, and the long sweep of the tail and the white beak. *If in Arizona a jaguar roams . . .*

I take out my notebook and sketch the darter, then just the outline of the dorsal fins.

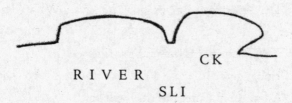

RIVER SLICK

*River: the leveling long sound and letter-balanced look*
*Slick: the bare back's slide before a sharp peak down*
*sight, sound, sense, word and word-for all made one*

The *nature* of words, like those strung to make Albion's leaf-woven alphabet. I imagine the river slick, its quick sails fullmasted in streamswift, currentkeeled then righted.

I close the notebook and place a hand on the poplar to get up. The lichen feels like old paint peeling, the bark itself all scrimshaw and scurf. Last week I'd brought children to the meadow. How many different things can you see? At first only three—tree, grass, flower—then as they moved around the meadow, actually *seeing*. Over a hundred before they left.

As I step out of the trees, a hollow crunch beneath my boot. Cicada slough. What a gift to shed one's old self so easily.

## *Twelve*

Jarvis and Barry were already changing when I joined them in the basement. I took off my shoes and slipped on the white Tyvek hazmat suit, zipped it up to my sternum. We looked like astronauts preparing for launch. After that I put on my steel-toed rubber boots and latex gloves. We got the duct tape and helped each other seal any possible gaps, because we'd be entering a place where, if they were cooking, just a few breaths could collapse a lung, numb your hands and feet, and do real nasty things to your central nervous system. We got our respirators and went out to the van, Jarvis driving, me beside him, and Barry in the back. Everyone was quiet, the only sound the AC running on high. Our faces beaded with sweat and it wasn't just from the suits. Bad memories traveled with us as well.

Jarvis had almost been stabbed with an HIV-infected needle. Barry's arm had been slashed by a kitchen knife. As for me, a broken nose and dislocated shoulder—and a loaded Ruger pistol aimed at my face. We also knew how a 9-millimeter Glock that would drop a regular human wouldn't stop a meth addict. They'd eat the lead and keep on coming. Which was why I always brought a 12-gauge riot gun. Even a meth head stepped back from a load of double-ought buckshot.

Beginning our descent into the valley, we entered National Forest land. There were no buildings or pavement like in Becky's park, just one old logging road and at its end a few campsites, the rest forest. After a hiker's complaint last April, I'd found green Mountain Dew bottles meth heads had used for shake and bake, some still leaking their poison. Syringes lurked in the broom sedge, needles awaiting more human flesh to puncture. Not exactly a scene to support Becky's views on nature bringing out the best in humans.

"Think we need to check it out again?" Jarvis asked, pointing at the logging road.

"Probably," I answered. "I'll run out here in the morning."

"I can do it," Jarvis said.

"No, you need to be at the courthouse getting used to being in charge."

The road leveled a last time and then plunged toward the valley floor. My mother's father had left the mountains as a teenager and found work as a sandhog on a bridge being built on the Mississippi. He'd told me how, as the wooden caisson descended, the water pressure thickened the blood in his veins. Eardrums and eyes felt ready to burst. Sometimes the pressure sprung nosebleeds. Something of that feeling came to me now as the mountains pressed tighter around us, squeezing out the sky. Because coming into this valley was also a descent into memory, my first meth bust and what had happened afterward.

When Rodney Greer's trailer came in sight, Jarvis turned on the blue light. We pulled into the yard and got out. It wasn't only the Tyvek that made us move slow. No one wanted to trip and fall where a needle might be. Barry yelled out, "Sheriff's department," and, Glock in hand, placed himself where he could see inside when the trailer door opened. I stood in the center of the yard with my shotgun while Jarvis, Glock ready as well, stepped up and tried the knob. It turned. Jarvis reached his arm out wide, and swung the door open. He looked at Barry and Barry nodded. Jarvis waited a few moments and peeked inside, then slowly went up the concrete steps, paused to pull his mask close to his mouth, and went inside.

"Both hands," Jarvis shouted, then waved us forward.

I went in next. As always, the seconds seemed to

widen. I felt the slickness of the linoleum under my feet. I heard the sound of breathing, my own but Jarvis's as well, soon Barry's as he came in behind me. The open door let in a wedge of midday light and the room emerged from the shadows. Music was playing. I didn't know the song but it was the Beach Boys.

Jarvis cuffed Rodney Greer and sat him on the couch where Ben Lindsey's daughter was passed out. She wore a green halter top and a pair of maroon sweatpants, no shoes. Every other toenail was painted black, like piano keys. A thin line of drool ran down the right side of her mouth. Television glamorized meth, even when they tried not to. You didn't smell the moldy food, or the vomit, shit, or blood, the meth itself burning your nose like ammonia, or how, once you'd arrested them, you turned your face so you didn't smell their rotting mouths. No, TV couldn't give you that.

I tapped her cheek, spoke, but got no response. Too soon I'd be passing the bad news on to Ben, something I'd done twice before.

The place was about what I'd expected. Dirty clothes were dumped beside the door. On the coffee table a pipe and lighter, a baggie half-full of crystal. Bunched-up snack wrappers, a soft drink can. A trash bag, one of the big plastic black ones, sagged beside the couch. It reeked so bad I smelled it through the respirator. Jarvis went into the back room while I checked the kitchen. Two needles with plastic syringes were on the counter. Another needle was on the floor beside an old-style microwave too long and wide to fit on the counter, its extension cord stretched tight as it reached up to a socket. But no ammonia bottles or lithium strips lying around. I figured if they were cooking, they were doing it somewhere else.

Jarvis came from the back room with another big trash bag, this one full. He turned it up and the contents spilled onto the floor. Batteries, brake fluid, red lye, coffee filters, bleach, and a dozen packs of Sudafed. All of it looked to be unopened.

"Expecting a bad allergy season, Greer?" I asked. "Or is it your year to be Santa Claus down here?"

Jarvis gave a chuckle but Barry was silent.

"Ain't none of that illegal," Greer answered.

"Was there a crib or bassinet back there?" I asked.

Jarvis said no and removed his respirator. He took a cautious sniff, then a deeper one.

"I don't think they've cooked here," Jarvis said.

I took off my respirator as well, but Barry, who still stood by the doorway, didn't. He had a three-year-old and a nine-month-old at home and was always more careful. When we got back to the courthouse, he'd shower and scrub every inch of himself with a washcloth he never used twice. The clothes he'd worn under the hazmat always went straight to the laundromat. A few months back I'd run into Carly, his wife, at the grocery store. She'd told me how upset Barry got if anything at home—toys, shoes, cups—wasn't kept in its proper place. Countertops had to be spotless, windowsills dusted. More than once after a meth raid, Barry had gotten up in the middle of the night and vacuumed every rug in the house. *It's what he sees in those meth houses that makes him that way*, Carly had told me.

"How much has she done?" I asked Rodney Greer.

"I ain't speaking another word till I'm lawyered up," Greer said.

I'd arrested him before, both times for simple possession. Like Darby Ramsey, Greer liked to play the tough guy but even drugged up he knew he was in deep shit now. I tapped the Lindsey girl's face again, hard enough to redden her cheek.

"Where's your baby?" I asked when her eyes opened.

"Baby?" she said, her eyes unfocused.

"Your baby," I said. "Is it at your parents' house?"

I asked twice more before she nodded toward the kitchen, muttered *in there*.

For a few moments no one breathed. It was like we believed if we were still enough that her words and their meaning might slide right past us and evaporate.

Barry took off his respirator.

"No," he said.

Just that one word. Then he reached under the Tyvek and unpinned his badge, laid it and the respirator beside the door, and walked down the concrete steps. Jarvis ran a gloved hand over his damp red hair but his feet could just as well have been nailed to the trailer floor. He wasn't going near the microwave either. *You're still sheriff,* I knew he was thinking as he met my eyes, *and I'm damn glad you are.*

The CD player was on the counter. I went to it first and hit the eject button. The disk slid out, ENDLESS SUMMER on the label. I set the disk on the counter and took a step into the kitchen. The syringe's needle was pointed toward me. I set my boot toe against the tip and kicked it into the opposite corner, then kneeled in front of the microwave, one hand touching the floor to hold my balance. The microwave door was a quarter open and a bit of pink cloth spilled out onto the kitchen floor. My free hand tugged the cloth and a blanket corner emerged. I let go and set my free hand on the floor as well, because I was suddenly unsteady. The trailer was silent, not even a clock tick or refrigerator hum.

*Even if it is, you can stand it,* I told myself. *You will leave this trailer and outside will be the same trees and the same roads and the same sky. The world will still be the world.* Then another thought came. *God help you if this is the vindication you've sought all of these years.*

I raised my gloved hand and settled my fingers on the door's edge. Sweat stung my eyes and I wiped a forearm across them, then across my brow. I told myself to get it over with, told myself twice.

Then from inside the microwave, not a cry or whimper but just a baby, a normal baby, letting the world know she was awake, maybe a bit hungry. I opened the microwave's door all the way. She lay on the scrunched-up blanket, a pacifier next to her cheek. I let go of a breath I'd not known I was holding, then lifted the baby and blanket out. I nodded for Jarvis to take the child. He tucked the pacifier in her mouth and went outside.

"We didn't harm a hair on that baby's head," Rodney Greer said. "Ain't none of you can claim different."

Ben Lindsey's daughter had closed her eyes again. After a raid last spring, a reporter asked me to describe what meth did to a person. Time-lapse photography on a human body, I'd answered, and here it was. She couldn't be over twenty-five but you'd have guessed forty. Sores pocked her matchstick arms, hair thin and greasy. The cheekbones jutted out and made the bottom half of her face, especially the mouth, seem to have caved in on itself. A tattoo bruised a forearm. Crudely done, a dog or horse, facing her hand with legs flexed, as if trying to flee. Her first name had slipped my mind, but then I remembered.

*Robin.*

Jarvis came back into the trailer.

"The SBI guys are here, Sheriff. They said since we had the baby, they'd take care of the notices and evidence. They saw Barry. He was walking back toward town."

Jarvis grabbed Greer by an arm and jerked him off the couch, and I helped Robin Lindsey to her feet. Outside, Barry's suit lay on the grass. He'd shed it like an insect's husk. We got Rodney Greer and Robin seated behind the mesh screen as SBI posted the bright yellow biohazard warnings. Jarvis and I stripped off the hazmat suits and stuffed them in the back with Barry's. I called Ruby to have her contact social services, decided to go ahead and have her call Ben as well. Jarvis sat in the passenger seat with the baby while I drove.

Barry was already a half-mile up the road. He wouldn't look at me or stop walking so I had to keep the van moving.

"The baby's all right," I told him. "She's fine. See, she's just sleeping. Come on, get in."

Barry stopped but he didn't get in. He was crying.

"I'm never going into a place like that again. I'll bag groceries or shovel shit before I do."

"I understand," I said, "but you can't walk all the way home. It's twelve miles."

"I will before I get in the van with them in it."

"Look, I'll call Carly and tell her to come pick you up, but at least get off the road in some shade and wait for her."

"I'm getting as far from that place as I can," Barry said and paused, met my eyes.

"What is it?" I asked.

"You were in there making jokes about it," Barry answered softly.

He started walking and I couldn't get him to stop or talk or look at me. I speed-dialed Carly and she said she'd drop their kids off at her mom's and get here quick as she could.

"Carly's coming," I told Barry, but he just kept walking.

For a while the van was silent, the baby asleep in Jarvis's arms, Robin and Greer silent in the back. As the road began its last ascent, we passed back through the National Forest land.

"If this baby . . . ," Jarvis said, breaking the silence, "if what we thought . . ."

"You're better off not thinking about that," I said.

"But if it had been . . ."

"It wasn't," I answered.

We were almost to town when a blue Escort swept past. I glimpsed Carly's frightened face. *Don't be*, I thought. *Be glad.*

I had still been a deputy when Sheriff Poston, me, and another deputy had returned from busting a biker and his girlfriend in this same valley. It had been at the beginning of the meth plague, though it was called crank back then.

There'd been a baby in that house too, stashed in a crib, wearing a diaper that hadn't been changed for days, the formula in the child's bottle rancid. The biker resisted and we all had scrapes and bruises, with it the fear of AIDS, because this was when the media's hysteria about HIV was at its peak. We'd finally gotten the biker and his girlfriend locked up in the back. The return ride had been a nightmare, the cat-piss reek on the prisoners and the baby, who wailed all the way. When I'd come into the main office, the dispatcher said Sarah had called three times since we'd left. I needed to call the moment I got in, Sarah had told her. *If you had seen what I saw today, what I had to deal with, instead of lounging in bed all afternoon, you'd have a damn reason to be depressed.* Those were the first words I'd said to Sarah on the courthouse's pay phone. The last, right before I'd slammed the phone back onto its cradle, *Go ahead and do it then.* Afterward, I'd joined the other deputy at Burrell's Taproom to wind down with a beer, the way I'd often done before going home to Sarah. But as soon as the first beer was in my hands, I got worried. I took one sip and left. As I drove down our street, I met the ambulance pulling out. I turned around, a siren chasing a siren all the way to the ER entrance. I'd watched them gurney Sarah from the ambulance and on inside the doors that said NO ENTRANCE.

*She's sedated, so she may not say much. It was damn close, Les. She'd be dead if your neighbor hadn't happened by.*

That's what Dr. Washburn had told me outside Sarah's room. Her eyes had opened when I entered but at first she seemed not to recognize me. Then Sarah had raised a hand that slowly curled inward before settling back on the sheet. *I guess neither of us got what we wanted*, she had said and closed her eyes again.

After Sarah had left the hospital, she'd gone to Hickory to live with her mother. Two months passed before we'd seen each other again. That afternoon, her mother stayed in the back of the house while Sarah and I talked in the front room. Sarah told me a doctor in Hickory had put her on a different antidepressant. "It was like a light coming on inside my head," she'd said. "I don't feel giddy or even happy, Les, just some hope. Maybe I'll be okay, but I can't know that for sure." I'd told Sarah how glad I was that she felt better. I told her I didn't want us to divorce, but she shook her head. No, she'd said. A divorce was best for both of us.

Sarah had walked me to the front door. She'd opened the door, then kissed my cheek. I'd smelled her perfume, her shampoo, felt her small ringless hand on my shoulder.

"What I said to you," I told her, putting my arms around her. "You know I didn't mean it."

"I know," Sarah had said softly, then just as softly freed herself from my embrace.

When I'd stepped out onto the porch, Sarah had closed the door slowly, tenderly.

# *Thirteen*

---

*Dragonflies* was the word Hopkins used, but my grand-parents called them what was believed: *snake doctors*. This one stream-hovering, its sun-saddled back greenshimmering, wings blurring like whitewater to still the piped body. I open my notebook to the NEW POEMS section and write

```
            s
doc         n         tor
            a
            k
            e
```

I imagine the insect about to settle on the snake's wounded flesh.

> *Minister whose idling cross-shadow blessed*
> *even before wings stilled and the virid touch*

Nothing else comes so I set the notebook beside me. What else is here? I listen. This section of stream purls and riffles amid small stones. What word might be made for what I hear? I pick up the notebook again, turn to a back page. First, I write *petrichor* and its definition.

> *petrichor: the smell of first raindrops on long-dry land.*

Then

> *petrichord: the sound of water sliding over smooth stone.*

I close the notebook and follow the stream to the bridge. In the pool's tailrace, a misplaced glinting. I peel off boots and socks, roll my pants. The stream's cold rises, each step a grainy give of sand. I lift a drink can, pour out the water. The sun at my back casts my shadow upstream. It touches the before of what I feel passing, like a memory of something that hasn't yet happened.

# *Fourteen*

At the courthouse, Jarvis handed the baby over to social services. He took Greer and Robin Lindsey downstairs to the jail, all the while Greer whining about a lawyer. I put the suits in the biohazard container and the respirators in the storage room, told Ruby to call Carly and check on Barry, then left for Greene's Café to get a sandwich and drink to go. As I came down the courthouse steps, Ben Lindsey pulled into the side lot. He got out of his pickup slowly, more like a man in his eighties than early fifties. Ben shut the driver's door the same way, the door not cleanly locking. He didn't bother to reclose it.

"Martha wouldn't come with me," Ben said. "That girl's own mother has given up on her, says the Robin we knew is dead and gone and ain't coming back. Her own mother thinking that way, Les, and I wish to God that I could too but I can't."

What was a man to say to that, especially one like me who'd never had a child? I told Ben that Robin was inside. He nodded and went on, taking each courthouse step slow as a man walking toward a noose.

In a county this rural, everyone's connected, if not by blood, then in some other way. In the worst times, the county was like a huge web. The spider stirred and many linked strands vibrated. When I entered the café the room got real quiet, which meant people already knew. A few conversations started back up, but they were soft, words exchanged about the weather or fishing, the sorts of things people spoke of when other things couldn't be.

But there are some who love nothing more than other people's misery. Bobbi Moffitt left her table, came over to where I waited by the cash register.

"It's a terrible thing, isn't it," she said. "Not for that girl but for Ben and Martha. They are such fine folks, Sheriff. I just don't know how they're able to go on after what that child has put them through. Of course, I've always been of a mind they didn't discipline her enough."

"Can you hurry up with that sandwich," I asked Lloyd, who nodded and went into the kitchen.

"Honestly, that girl was allowed to run wild. As

much as I hate to say it, I knew something like this was bound to happen. I'm sure you did too."

No one else in the room spoke now, no sound but the click of the ceiling fan's chain.

"I'm just concerned for them is all," Bobbi Moffitt said, and returned to her table.

I'd planned to eat in the office, but instead I walked to the park and sat at a picnic table, one no one else was near.

Spend a long period of time alone, especially if you're someone who's never been that social to begin with, and you find yourself craving solitude. After my divorce, I quit going by Burrell's Taproom after work and ate almost all of my meals at home or behind a closed office door. People in town accepted the change, maybe because they knew what had happened, not just the divorce but Sarah's overdose, or maybe because, after a while, folks in small towns quit noticing or caring about a person's eccentricities. You could walk around town with black scuba fins on your feet and a tiara on your head and people would soon quit caring or noticing. Like my painting watercolors, the inwardness was seen as a bit peculiar, but I was still a good sheriff.

It was my sisters who'd tried to draw me out after the divorce. They both lived in Alabama and offered to pay for my flights if I'd come visit, but I'd been curt enough that they'd quit offering, or calling. After a year, I went out on a few dates, but most times I couldn't wait to get back home and be alone. There had been, and sometimes still were, days I turned my head or crossed the street to avoid talking to someone. Even to acknowledge them with a nod drained me.

*Accomplices.*

When I returned to the office, my phone was blinking. I recognized the number as Jink Hampton's. He'd left no message but he didn't need to. The call itself was the message—he had his monthly "tithe," as he called it, and was ready for me to pick it up.

But before driving out to Jink's place, I called Becky. It was good to hear her voice, so good in fact that I told her so. She asked about the raid, and I told her it went no worse than we'd expected. I left it at that and asked how Gerald was.

"I'm doing what Dr. Washburn told me, making sure the scrapes stay disinfected. What that guard did," Becky said, her voice beginning to tremble. "What could have happened . . ."

"It *was* wrong," I said, "but Gerald shouldn't have been at the waterfall or the resort. I know he's used to things being different, but it is Tucker's property. You've got to make Gerald understand that. You're the only person he's going to listen to."

"I know," Becky said.

"Listen," I said, "if you have a free minute, can you see if C.J. Gant's SUV is in the resort's lot? It's the light blue one. Tucker was really ticked off at him yesterday. I don't think he'd do anything like fire C.J., but I want to be sure."

"It will be fifteen minutes before I can," Becky said. "I'll call you back when I know."

"I'll be driving so call me on my cell phone," I said. "Thanks."

"I'm glad you're okay," Becky said softly. "I worried about you."

"I'm fine."

I told Ruby I'd be out of the office for the rest of the day.

"What about Barry?" she asked. "I can't get an answer at his house or on his cell."

"I'll try him tonight," I said.

As I drove out to Jink Hampton's place, I told myself again that Harold Tucker wouldn't fire C.J., even if the resort did need to lay off some people. It came down to loyalty, many years of it. My cell phone buzzed.

"His SUV is in the parking lot," Becky said.

"Thanks," I said. "We're still on for lunch Friday, right?"

"As long as Gerald is okay," Becky said.

It had been in ninth grade when Mr. Ketner, the principal, announced during homeroom that my watercolor had been chosen to represent our school in a state-wide competition. Eric Dalton, who'd failed ninth grade twice, turned to his buddies on the back row. *That's almost as faggy as writing poetry,* he'd said. His buddies laughed loudly, in part because Eric was not just the biggest ninth-grader but the meanest. When the rest of the class turned to look at him, Eric stared back. *What I said was funny, wasn't it?* he challenged. C.J. was on the front row. Not even a laugh was necessary, just a smile and he'd be, maybe for the first time in his life, on the other side of the taunts, invited into the safety of the herd. When the laughs rippled to the front row, C.J. didn't even smile, and he didn't look at me. He turned to the front of the room and waited for the teacher to restore order.

Four months later he would save my life.

Jink Hampton raised dope but he also bred Plott hounds. When I got to his house, he led me inside the pen, picked up a pup from a new litter. It had the right brindled coloring and the rambunctiousness that usually predicted an adult that would be tireless on the trail.

"You in the market for a good bear dog?" Jink asked. "Since you're retiring you'll be needing a hobby, won't you?"

"I'm thinking more along the lines of a garden."

Jink smiled.

"I've got some good Early Misty seeds if you want them."

"I think I'll stick to corn and tomatoes, maybe some squash," I said. "Any helicopters flown around here this week?"

"Nah," Jink answered. "I heard they been flying over government land though."

"You know they'll spread out since it's harvest time."

"I know," Jink said, and grimaced as he took a fifty-dollar bill from his wallet. "I reckon this will help buy you another window."

"Maybe so," I said, and stuffed the bill in my pocket.

Jink set the pup down and came out of the pen.

"How is your cabin coming along?" Jink asked. "I reckon I ought to know since I'm financing it."

"The well is in and the road graded and graveled. They started the foundation. After I leave here I'm going by to check."

"Well, it's a pretty piece of land."

"It is," I said.

For a few moments we watched the pups play tug-of-war with a strip of cowhide.

"I don't guess you have an idea who Darby Ramsey might buy meth from?" I asked.

"You know I don't have any truck with meth, or Oxy either."

"I do know that," I said, "just thought you might have heard something."

"No, but I heard about Gerald's tussle yesterday. You didn't law him, did you?"

"No."

"Good, I wouldn't want trouble for that old man. Me and his boy William was tight as tree bark growing up. I never had a better friend then nor now. Hard to believe Darby comes from the same stock, ain't it?"

"It is."

"I know you're not supposed to go back on your word," Jink said, "especially when you give it to your sister on her deathbed, but damned if I'd let Darby inherit anything I left behind. You know he'll spend every dime of it on drugs."

"I do," I said, and took the car keys from my pocket. "Anyway, you got a fine litter there."

"They should be, but dogs are like people. No matter how good the bloodline, they can still turn out sorry."

We walked over to my car.

"So this is the last time between me and you," Jink said.

"This is it."

"What about Jarvis Crowe? Do I have the same arrangement with him?"

"I don't know," I said. "That's between you and Jarvis."

"You ever talked to him about it?"

"I haven't, but you and I both know he's wise to what's going on. If he wants it to continue he'll drop by."

"Hell, Les, what if he 'drops by' just to arrest my ass?"

"Like I said, you boys will have to work it out."

"All right," Jink said, extending his hand. "Have a good retirement."

# *Fifteen*

---

*At ten tonight come to the I-81 rest stop, the one between the two Emory exits. R.*

The note had been placed under the park truck's wiper blade. This was six months after I'd moved out, two weeks before Richard died. By then he was being sought for setting fire to a mine owner's house. A homegrown terrorist, newspapers said, another Ted Kaczynski. Don't go, a part of me said, but I went.

The first interstate sign with the word EMORY was like a knife tip touching my stomach. A dull knife, but each time EMORY appeared, eighteen miles, ten miles, four, the blade pressed deeper. I turned off the highway and parked. Where my parents' house had been, where the elementary school still was—all were within a mile. No other vehicle was at the rest stop, but minutes later a jeep pulled in beside me. A man I didn't know got out.

"Hand me your cell phone," he said, and took out the battery and threw it into the woods.

"Wait here," he said, then got in the jeep and drove off.

"They don't even notice it anymore, do they?"

I turned around and Richard was coming out of the woods.

"I mean the exhaust," he said. "They think air is supposed to smell like poison."

Richard came closer, about to draw me to him, but I stepped back.

"No?" he asked.

I shook my head.

"You always were a different kind of person that way," Richard said. "*Noli me tangere* one day, not even a kiss, then another day not so. That's okay. These last few months, I understand more and more why you're that way. People take too much from you, don't they? You have to pull away awhile, keep the contagion at a minimum and only then with a few kindred spirits."

"Why did you want me to come here?" I asked.

Richard didn't answer, just motioned for me to follow him away from the lights to sit at a concrete picnic table.

For a few moments the only sound was the whoosh of passing cars.

"This was risky for me," Richard said, "but I had to see you."

He raised his hand, traced the fall of my hair down my shoulders. Memories of sleeping bags and beds and meadows rushed back. My body wanted to lean into that touch. The ache of so long not having.

"I'm glad you haven't cut it," Richard said. He let his fingertips brush slowly down my spine, touching my jeans before he removed his hand. "I want you to come with me. Six months since the verdict and not a word about a retrial. The bastards can even kill kids and get away with it, Becky. Change comes only from my way. It always does in the end."

"That house you burned down, children could have been inside," I said. "That late at night you couldn't have been certain no one was there."

"If that bastard's kids had been there, their blood would be on his hands, not mine. The Bible's got that right if nothing else. *The sins of the father . . .*"

The jeep came up the exit ramp and parked. The engine stayed on, but the driver got out and waited.

"Why meet, why here?"

"You mean Emory?"

"Yes."

"To free you from this place forever and start again, Becky," Richard said. "You can leave here with me, no longer a victim of anything or anyone in your past. Come with me, tonight. Even if the worst happens, at least you won't be a victim. I'm giving you a choice of which to be, Becky, maybe for the only time in your life. You're not stupid. You've seen enough to know my way is the only one that will work."

"I can't believe that," I answered.

"Yes, you can, but it has to be now. Soon we won't have any chance. They've got the technology in place. In five years people won't even know they're in the world, much less care about what happens to it. They will believe that when everything else on this planet dies, they'll be able to disappear into a computer screen. They believe it *now*, most of them."

For a few moments there was only silence.

"What you're saying," I answered. "If I let myself believe that, I couldn't endure living."

Richard reached for my hand but I clasped both of mine tight and stood.

"I need to go," I said and walked back to the lot, Richard following.

"You want me to cut the cord on her CB?" the jeep driver asked.

"No," Richard answered.

"You certain?"

"Unless Becky tells me otherwise."

Richard met my eyes.

"If a child had been in the house I burned down, you'd have turned me in, or tried to, wouldn't you?"

"Yes."

Richard nodded and got in the jeep. As it was pulling out, he smiled and said something but the jeep's engine drowned it out. Probably just a good-bye.

After he died, I'd packed provisions for two weeks and gone deep into Shenandoah National Park, followed the trails leading to what was farthest away. Where the trails ended, I went beyond, pushed through a gorge of laurel slicks and over a ridge where I set up camp. One afternoon I'd wandered the woods, found an old homestead with its cairn of chimney rocks. There the fox grape's musky odor thickened the air. Yellow bells and periwinkle spread untended. How many decades such silence, I had wondered, what last words were spoken before the people left. I'd walked back to my camp and opened the only book I'd brought. I settled the poems inside of me one at a time. First "The Windhover," and then "Pied Beauty," by the end of the next week a dozen more. Letting Hopkins' words fill the inner silence. *Inscape of words.* A new language to replace the old one I no longer could interpret.

I close the park gate and leave, try to lock away memory as well. I need to check on Gerald but pedal toward the Parkway first, feel the release of being in a body all-aware.

A mown hay field appears, its blond stubble blackened by a flock of starlings. As I pass, the field seems to lift, peek to see what's under itself, then resettle. A pickup passes from the other direction. The flock lifts again and this time keeps rising, a narrowing swirl as if sucked through a pipe and then an unfurl of rhythm sudden sprung, becoming one entity as it wrinkles, smooths out, drifts down like a snapped bedsheet. Then swerves and shifts, gathers and twists. *Murmuration*: ornithology's word-poem for what I see. Two hundred starlings at most, but in Europe sometimes ten thousand, enough to punctuate a sky. What might a child see? A magic carpet made suddenly real? Ocean fish-schools swimming air? The flock turns west and disappears.

## *Sixteen*

As I drove back toward town, I thought of what Jink had said about Darby and his bloodline, but it could go the other way too. My dad had been as kind and gentle a man as I've ever known. He'd never laid a hand on me, even when my mother argued that he should. But my father's father had been a monster. He'd come home drunk and slap my grandmother around, then jerk his belt off and flail the backs of my father and his younger brother. Until one night when Dad was fourteen. The old man had staggered through the front door and my father swung a ball bat as hard as he could into my grandfather's kneecap. He'd fallen and Dad and his brother beat him senseless and then dragged him out of the house and all the way to the road. They told their father if he ever came back they'd kill him. He'd hobbled away and no one ever saw him again.

A lot of men couldn't get past such childhoods though. They'd stay trapped in the same cycle. I'd seen it too often. The boys with welts and bruises from their fathers' belts and fists would do the same to their own wives and children, becoming the very thing they'd feared and hated most growing up. After my parents' deaths, I'd found a single photograph with my grandfather in it. His eyes didn't look at the camera or at his family standing beside him. Instead, they'd gazed toward something to his right, as if denying any connection. I'd studied his features, found more of me in them than I had wished.

I hadn't thought anyone to be around this late, but as I came up the freshly graveled road Billy Orr's truck was parked in front of the cabin's foundation. He sat in the cab, the driver's window down. I pulled up beside him.

"Just come by to see how far they got today," Billy said. "It's coming along good, don't you think?"

"I do."

"Matter of fact, I'm ready to order the porch materials. You're still sure you want that wrap around, the one I showed you?"

"I am."

"It'll give you a pretty view in four directions," Billy

said, his gaze sweeping the mountains now, "but like I said, counting labor, it'll be around twenty-five thousand."

"That's fine," I answered. "I need to go ahead and pay you, for everything. A hundred and twenty-five thousand total, right?"

"That's right, but pay half now and half when it's finished. I want you to be certain you're satisfied."

"All right. I'll get half to you by Monday. It'll be cash."

"I'm not averse to real money," Billy said, smiling as he cranked the engine. "If something's not the way you want it, let me know."

After Billy left, I checked out the foundation. Everything looked plumb, no cracks or bulges, the end and bed joints precisely measured. No drink bottles or food wrappers left behind either, another sign that Billy's crew took pride in their work. I turned and looked at the view I'd have from the front porch. In winter, I'd see a couple of second homes on the ridge, but for now it was green trees and blue mountains and silence.

It was a scene I'd once enjoyed viewing with a brush in my hand and a blank canvas. After a day dealing with the usual messes, it was nice to set an easel outdoors and look at the mountains, then try to re-create them, mixing colors to get the right shade of a leaf or boulder, or capture the way a tree limb reached crookedly toward the sky. The pleasure of that quietness, because even if people saw me in a yard or field they'd leave me be. Plus the pride anybody gets from doing something well, as the county art show ribbons attested, though sometimes, less proudly, an excuse to get away from Sarah. Which was ironic, because, like a lot of things, I'd not enjoyed painting much after she was gone, and so quit.

I walked back to the car but didn't get in. I leaned against the hood and looked at the mountains. A breeze stirred as the sun began to sink below them. Soon the leaves on the hardwoods would turn. *Like the mountains are huddled under a big crazy quilt.* That was what my grandmother used to say when it happened. *Crazy quilt.* It was an expression you rarely heard these days, same as "Proud to know you," or "It's a gracious plenty." I thought about Gerald, who understood those words but, in a deeper way, couldn't understand a NO TRESPASSING sign, because it belonged to a world he didn't know.

I had been bad to sleepwalk as a kid. There were times, for some reason always in the summer, I'd make my way out of the house and end up in the yard. Folks back then, or at least country folks, didn't see the need for a porch bulb burning all night. I'd open my eyes and there'd be nothing but darkness, like the world had slipped its leash and run away, taking everything with it except me. Then I'd hear a whip-poor-will or a jar fly, or feel the dew dampening my feet, or I'd look up and find the stars tacked to the sky where they always were, only the moon roaming.

I turned onto the main road and drove back toward town, all the while remembering what it had felt like when the world you knew had up and vanished, and you needed to find something to bring that world back, and you weren't sure that you could.

# PART THREE

PART THREE

## Seventeen

We were at Laurel Fork, not just Sarah and me but with three children, who soon left the water to get warm. Sarah joined them. They lay sprawled on the big boulder while I stood above the waterfall. Can you touch the bottom? Sarah asked me. I dove and when I surfaced Sarah and the children were gone. Only damp shadows remained.

Then the phone was ringing. I looked over at the clock and saw it was 8:20.

"Harold Tucker just called," Ruby said. "He said you need to get out to the resort right now. You, not a deputy. I sent Jarvis but Mr. Tucker was adamant that you come too."

I got dressed and drove to the resort, already thinking that whatever had happened, Gerald was involved. Becky's truck was parked next to C.J.'s SUV, another bad sign.

She and Jarvis were down by the creek and I joined them. Becky kneeled beside the stream, filling a plastic bottle with water. A few yards farther, where the culvert was, a brown trout, easily five pounds, drifted against the mesh wire. More dead trout were around it.

"What in the hell happened?" I asked.

"A fish kill," Jarvis answered. "They say it is worse upstream where there's a big waterfall. DENR's on the way. They've already contacted the water treatment plant and they've shut down the intake valves."

"It's that bad?"

"They're just being safe, same as us," Becky said. "There are no dead fish in the park, but Carlos is posting warning signs."

"It smells like diesel fuel," I said.

"It's kerosene," Jarvis said.

He pointed at the reddish sheen on a pool's edge. But it wasn't just there. Red tinged a sandbar upstream, as if the creek was bleeding.

"Why do you say that?" Becky asked, turning from the water she now tested.

"They put red dye in kerosene," I said, "to differentiate it from on-road diesel."

Becky didn't look pleased to hear that. She already knew where this was leading.

"What do your tests say?" I asked.

"The ammonia levels aren't elevated, right here at least."

"Which means?"

"It's probably not organic or animal waste and I don't smell a herbicide," Becky said. "Sewage or a pesticide either. But we won't have the results for at least a week."

"But isn't it obvious what killed them?" Jarvis said. "I mean, you can smell it, and the red."

"There could be something else mixed with it," Becky said. "Or some chemical that was added in diesel fuel."

"I'm just saying," Jarvis added.

But Becky ignored him. She set the last sample bottle in the tackle box and snapped it shut.

"Where's Tucker?" I asked Jarvis.

"Inside making phone calls."

"You talk to him?"

"Just for a few moments. He was waiting for you to come. Mr. Tucker said this was done on purpose. He says he damn well knows who did it."

"I'm going upstream," Becky said, getting up, "to try and find where it was introduced."

I watched her walk up the trail and disappear into the woods.

*She already knows*, I thought, *but she doesn't want to hear it.*

"So Tucker thinks Gerald did this?"

"He didn't say Gerald's name but you know that's

what he's thinking." Jarvis shook his head and frowned. "It's not much of a stretch to think so."

"No," I said, as Harold Tucker came out on the lodge's porch and motioned me toward him. "It isn't."

"I've got something to show you, Sheriff," Tucker said.

## *Eighteen*

As I move upstream, vomit scalds my throat like lye. Trout shoal on sandbars and banks. A few gills quiver feebly but most fish are death-paled, browns and rainbows now in name only. Festering sores on streamskin. Dace and war-paint shiners are sprinkled amid the larger fish. Two buzzards stalk the shallows, more overhead, blackly circling like clock hands. The stream rises and narrows. A dead trout vanes in the eddy. On the trail, between two stems of ironweed, a writing spider sways in the web's palm. One eyelash-thin leg poised, as if pausing before finishing its message.

**T? R? G?**

Gerald couldn't do this. *I know him.* This *isn't* like it was with Richard.

The stream disappears into rhododendron, then sidles back close as the trail dips before rising again. I hear the waterfall and soon after I emerge behind it. A wreath of dead fish circle the pool. Here salamanders and crayfish awash too. The fuel smells stronger, and more red stains appear on the sand and water. It's dye you are seeing, nothing more, I remind myself, but what I see feels like blood.

I walk on up above the falls, where a granite bald pushes back trees to open the sky. Dead trout are here as well, all native. *I didn't likely think any of them speckled trout were still around but one day I was up here and I seen one,* Gerald had said last fall, pointing into the water at one speckled trout and then another as we'd made our way upstream to a last pool before the creek split. I push through leathery rhododendron leaves to that same pool. A speckled trout fins in the center, another in the shallows. They look perfectly healthy so I retrace my steps, find a stain on the granite twenty yards from the waterfall. I rub the dampness with my fingers. Viscous. I raise it to my nose and it all comes back.

We'd hidden behind the school buses that morning. Fuel had been spilled and I'd smelled it, felt it under my shoe soles. Then the policeman rushed us from behind the buses and across the black pavement. Some of us were screaming and then more screams when ambulances splashed red across our shirts and blouses. The policeman shouted, *It's only red light, children, only light,* herding us onto the grass where too many hands grabbed as flash-bulbs burst like the hallway's first loud flash.

The first loud flash . . .

*Promise me, children, not a single word,* Ms. Abernathy had whispered, then led us down the hallway single file to the basement doorway. Then the cave feel of tight walls leading to a cool darkening. I am the very last, reaching for Ms. Abernathy's hand as we make our way to the concrete floor. So much silence, the only sound pipedrip. Light slants down from the stair entrance. Ms. Abernathy ushers us toward the light leaking in from the basement door. Almost there when her *shhhhh* stills us. Footsteps come halfway down the stairs and pause. Both my hands clutch Ms. Abernathy's. Another footstep and a shoe and pants cuff appear. The pipe drips loud and my first tears well. I try to squeeze the tears back inside me but the first one falls and I know he has heard it. . . . *Ms. Abernathy stands in the basement door, blocking the exit as I run. Close your eyes, a policeman says as he grabs me. But I look back and when I do my tongue turns to salt.*

# *Nineteen*

---

"Video was taken up at the waterfall this morning," Tucker told me, "where my workers found the first dead fish."

Randall Cobb, one of Tucker's security team, tapped a few buttons. The screen changed to black and white and the back of a head passed in front of the camera's lens.

"That was 7:51 A.M. and this next one is 8:34," Tucker said.

Randall punched a few more buttons. I could see the face this time, blurry but unmistakable.

"You're acting surprised, Sheriff."

"It's just that I can't see him doing this."

"You just *did* see it," Tucker snapped, "and I don't get why you're surprised. Gerald Blackwelder's gotten away with everything but poisoning my stream. Why would he figure he couldn't do that too?"

"Are other cameras up there?"

"There's another one fifty yards downstream."

"Have you checked it?"

"Why in hell do we need to?"

"Just to be sure no one else was up there."

"Check that other camera between midnight and ten A.M. and let the sheriff know if anyone's on it," Tucker told Randall. "Do it quick."

"Yes, sir."

Tucker didn't wear his golf clothes today. He had on a blue cotton suit, dress shoes, a white shirt but no tie. Perhaps it lay on his office desk or even the floor, unknotted then jerked off his collar when he heard what had happened. His frustration became more evident as we stepped outside and saw that a TV news van had pulled into the lot.

"DENR's already supposed to be here," Tucker fumed. "I can't clean up this mess till they say so. I've got phone calls to make, Sheriff. My hope is you or your deputy's gone to arrest Gerald Blackwelder before I finish them."

"Let's see what the second camera shows," I said, "but if you or C.J. talk to any newspeople, I'd appreciate you not mentioning Gerald by name until he's been charged."

"I'll be the one talking to them," Tucker said. "I fired C.J. Monday, after Gerald came and threatened me."

"You fired him?" I said. "But his SUV's here."

"I gave him two weeks' notice. But after this," Tucker said, gesturing at the creek, "I told him to clean out his office and leave, which he's doing now."

"But he couldn't have stopped this," I said, "or what happened Monday either."

"You're wrong about that," Tucker snapped. "Here's the difference between you and me, Sheriff. Unlike you, I don't wait for things to get out of hand before I act."

"But to fire him—"

"Look," Tucker interrupted. "C.J. asked me not to talk about him losing his job. I don't even know if he's told his family, though they'll surely know now."

"C.J.'s been too good an employee for you to do this."

Tucker glared at me.

"You had your role in this fiasco too, Sheriff. If you'd locked up Gerald on Monday, this fish kill wouldn't have happened."

Tucker turned and went into the lodge. As I left the porch, a news crew met me. I told the reporter, "No comment," and walked down the esplanade to where Jarvis waited.

"They've got Gerald on a security camera, right up there where the fish started dying."

"I guess we ought not be too surprised, but somehow I still am," Jarvis said. "You want me to go get him?"

"I'll do it, but not yet."

Tucker's security guard came and said no one was on the other camera, which pretty much sealed it. I looked at the big brown trout and thought of the one C.J. and I had tried to catch the summer of our junior year. *You're smart, Les, but you try to hide it.* But C.J. never hid his smarts. The taunts picked back up some as we entered our last two years of high school. *Teacher's pet, brownnoser.* Neither was true. Some of the teachers didn't like C.J. either, because at times he wasn't above questioning what they said in class. But after that day at his great-uncle's farm, I'd sit with him if I saw him alone in the cafeteria or at an assembly. He'd tried to get me to take college prep courses with him, even said we could study together. When C.J. had come back five years ago, he'd made it a point to tell me that the stay would be temporary, but in the last couple of years he hadn't said much about leaving, and I'd wondered if what my grandfather had told me was true, that if you're born in the mountains, you can't feel at home anywhere else. But now . . .

Becky came out of the woods, the tackle box in her right hand.

"That old man means a lot to her, doesn't he, Sheriff?" Jarvis said.

"Yes, he does," I answered, "and I'm afraid she's made

herself believe he's someone that he's not. Why don't you check in with Ruby while I talk to her."

"Okay," Jarvis said.

*You warned her about Gerald and now he's proven you right. The fault is with her, not you.* But that thought did me no good, especially because last night, in one of those 3 A.M. moments when we're most honest with ourselves, I'd wondered if in some way I'd known on Monday that Gerald would go to the resort and confront Tucker. *No,* I told myself, *I hadn't known that. I'd made Gerald promise that he wouldn't go. This is all Gerald's fault.* But it was like putting a metal washer in a vending machine and it falling straight into the change box. That same hollow ring.

"I found where it was introduced," Becky said as she joined me. "It's right above the waterfall."

"Did that confirm what it is?"

"Kerosene," Becky said, not meeting my eyes. "Some was spilled on the sand, but something else could have been dumped in."

"But you've got no cause to think something else was?"

"I can't say that for certain," Becky said. "Nobody can without the sample results."

"But kerosene," I said, pitching the word back to her like a baseball, "that's definite."

I waited but knew I'd have to be the one who said it. I stepped closer, placed my arm gently around her.

"You know this doesn't look good for Gerald. I mean, we both know he's got a temper."

"Gerald didn't do this," Becky said firmly as she would if I'd misidentified a wildflower.

"A camera at the waterfall shows him up there this morning. I saw the film and it's Gerald."

Becky's expression didn't change.

"They're showing some film they took on Monday."

"He's wearing a different shirt, Becky," I said softly.

"Gerald didn't do this."

"I know how much you care about Gerald," I said, "and I know some of it, probably a lot of it, has to do with your grandparents, what they did for you. But what you owe them, or feel you owe Gerald, has limits."

"Trout were killed above the waterfall, Les, speckled trout," Becky said, more emotion in her voice now. "I went up there with Gerald to look at them last fall. If you'd been with us that morning . . . if you had, you'd know he couldn't do this. Those speckled trout, Gerald didn't want to catch them to eat. He wanted them just to *be* there, and to stay there," Becky said, her voice breaking. "The way Gerald looked at those speckled trout. Les, he *loved* them."

*He loved his son too, but that didn't stop Gerald from burning his son's house down, with kerosene.* That's what I could have said, but instead I withdrew my arm and motioned toward Jarvis and Harold Tucker, who were coming to join us. Tucker had taken off the coat and rolled up his shirtsleeves. He looked ready to dig a ditch or enter a brawl. Whatever it took to straighten out the mess in the creek before him.

"So what did your tests tell you?" Tucker asked Becky.

"Kerosene's a transient phenomenon," Becky answered.

"What the hell does that mean?"

"Kerosene's not very water soluble so most of the damage has been done. DENR will probably issue a drinking water advisory but that may be just a precaution."

"And until they decide to show up?" Tucker asked.

"We're already putting warning flyers streamside at the park," Becky said. "You should do the same."

"For the first time all summer, I've got full capacity this weekend," Tucker fumed. "These people will want to fish, not worry that the water will poison them."

"It could have been a lot worse," I said.

"So it's just kerosene?" Jarvis asked.

"It's kerosene," Becky said, "but there could still be something else introduced with it."

"Kerosene dumped at the waterfall," Tucker said.

"Above the waterfall," Becky said, "at least fifty yards."

A droning came from above, quickly became a metallic clamor.

"Shit," Tucker shouted as a white helicopter, NEWS 5 on the side, hovered above the lodge. A cameraman leaned out to film, and then the helicopter flew away. "I've called DENR three times and they still aren't here but everyone else except goddamn *Sixty Minutes* is."

Tucker's eyes remained on the sky, where buzzards resumed their slow circling. Like a nightmare merry-go-round, I thought, and it was clear from Tucker's face he didn't find it an appealing sight either.

"That's another nice welcome," Tucker seethed. "Turn left when you see the buzzards. Go do your job, Sheriff. If you had on Monday when Gerald came up here raising hell—"

"He just wanted to talk to you," Becky said angrily. "Gerald didn't threaten anyone until your thugs came after him. And he didn't kill your fish, Mr. Tucker. I know Gerald and I know he wouldn't do this."

Tucker placed a hand on his cheek, rubbed upward, touching the hearing aid before adjusting his glasses. Doing it unconsciously, but it seemed a wish that all he'd heard and seen was not real but an equipment failure.

"I've known Gerald Blackwelder a lot longer than you, ma'am," Tucker said, "and I've seen a side of him maybe you haven't and I'm not even talking about his burning a house down. Long before he did that, I watched him nearly kill a man in a bar fight. Gerald knocked him to the floor and the guy didn't get up, couldn't get up, but Gerald kept punching him in the face, even after the guy was out cold. I was across the room and I could *hear* the teeth breaking. It took three fellows to get Gerald off him. That man he beat up was in the hospital a week. He lost half his teeth and the vision in his right eye. He would have been in a coffin if Gerald hadn't been stopped. So don't tell me I don't know the man, or what he can or can't do."

"Okay," I said, stepping in front of Tucker. "You can go back to the lodge. I'm going to go get Gerald now."

"Good," Tucker said, "and about damn time."

"Do you want me as backup?" Jarvis asked as Tucker stalked off.

"No, it's better if I go alone."

"You're going to arrest Gerald?" Becky asked, following me as I walked to the parking lot.

"*Detain*'s a better word."

"It means the same thing."

"Maybe it does," I said, getting tired real fast of people telling me what to do, "but it's what has to be done."

"It's wrong to do this to him, Les," Becky said.

*Nowhere near as wrong as C.J. getting fired,* I thought, seeing C.J.'s SUV in the lot.

I was about to get in the car when Becky grabbed my sleeve.

"His heart," Becky said. "I need to be there. You know I do."

"Drive your own vehicle then."

Becky didn't let go of my sleeve.

"Don't you understand that Gerald didn't do this, Les? I don't care what Tucker says. Gerald *couldn't* do this."

"Maybe you're wrong about what he's capable of," I said. Then more words blurted out before I could stop them. "You've been wrong before about what a person could do."

Becky flinched and let go of my sleeve. For the first time since we'd known each other, I'd hurt her. *Yes*, I thought. *Maybe it's not just Pelfrey and Gerald you are wrong about.*

When we drove up, Gerald was sitting on the porch, coffee mug in hand, and wearing the same shirt he had on in the video. He smiled and stood.

"Well, I'd not have reckoned a visit from you all this morning."

I stopped at the front step but Becky went up to stand beside him. She trembled but Gerald didn't seem to notice. He nodded at the helicopter droning above the ridge.

"Looking for dope, I reckon," he said. "Come up and warm a chair, Sheriff. I've got coffee enough for the three of us."

"You go ahead and finish that coffee," I said. "You and me need to go to the courthouse."

"What for?" Gerald asked, his head tilting slightly, brow furrowed.

"It's just a misunderstanding," Becky said, taking Gerald's free hand. "Someone poured kerosene into Locust Creek and killed a lot of trout."

"At the park?" Gerald asked.

"No," Becky said. "On Tucker's property, above the waterfall."

"And they think I done it?" Gerald asked after a few moments.

"They've got you on video, Gerald," I said. "Let's go."

"I never dumped anything in that creek," Gerald stammered.

"I know that," Becky told him, her other hand on his forearm now. "It'll get cleared up soon, it will."

The porcelain cup slipped from Gerald's hand. Coffee splashed on the porch but the cup didn't shatter.

"Becky," Gerald said, shaking his head as he spoke. "I'd not hurt them trout. You know that."

The helicopter must have seen my patrol car, because as I stepped onto the porch it skimmed over the last trees, raising dust and buffeting our clothes.

"We've got to go," I shouted.

I went and took Gerald's free arm. Becky and I got

him down the steps as grit lifted, stinging our eyes. The brown cloud thickened, gained twigs and pebbles. A plastic bag flapped against my leg, then gusted away. Coughing, Becky and I guided Gerald with one hand while shielding our eyes with the other. Gerald stumbled and almost caused us all to fall. The helicopter kept descending as if trying to drag the sky itself down upon us.

I got the back passenger door open and helped Gerald inside. As I did, Gerald slapped at his shirt pocket and Becky scrambled into the backseat. She cradled his head and took the pill bottle from his overalls pocket. She opened it, pressed a tablet into Gerald's mouth, then one more. Dust had powdered Becky's face and now tears streaked pale rivulets down her cheeks. I got in, turned on the blue light, and sped toward the hospital.

"Please, Gerald," Becky shouted, "please."

*He's going to die right in front of her,* I thought, glancing in the rearview mirror as we passed the resort.

"Tell me you're okay," Becky kept pleading, "at least open your eyes."

As we turned off the Parkway and headed toward town, Gerald responded, and the next time I glanced in the mirror much of the ashy grayness had left his face.

"You're going to be okay, Gerald," Becky kept saying, again and again.

*Yes, he will,* I thought when the hospital came in sight, and I wondered if in the coming days Gerald, and maybe all of us, would wish Becky hadn't given him the nitro tablets, and that he'd died in the arms of the one person left on earth who loved him.

## *Twenty*

The day of Grandmother's funeral, I'd entered the farmhouse alone. Sepia and mote drift, her absence all luster now gone. The sadness of a bowl left on a counter, a pair of reading glasses beside a chair. Something of that as I enter Gerald's house. But Gerald will return. The EKG fine, the overnight stay just precaution. *I didn't lock up the house*, Gerald mumbled as the IV drip eased him asleep. Everything inside looks okay, so I close the door and twist the key until the lock clicks.

Jarvis Crowe's patrol car is parked in Gerald's driveway. He searches where Gerald's pasture borders resort property. He'll check the barn, if he already hasn't, and find the kerosene can. But it will not be empty, I assure myself. *If you go to the barn and check, you doubt Gerald too.*

Instead, I take the canning jar I brought with me to the springhouse. The dipper dangles from a cherry tree limb. *The best water in this county*, Gerald swears. Mineral rich, but Gerald claims the cherry tree's roots sweeten it too. I lift the tin spring guard and fill the jar, twist the lid tight and set it on the ground. I scoop up a dipperful for myself, savor the chill passing into my chest as my nose inhales the after-rain smell of moss. When I place the tin back, I see a mud puppy, thready red gills fanning.

As I walk back, MASON brailles my palm and all is brought back: clay floor cool under my feet, dusky potato smell, the pint and quart jars floating above me, grandmother's tall hand lifting one down. You carry this one, she said. Even in the dim light the honey glowed, sunshine steeped in earthy blackness.

To be there with her in that dark place and know I was safe.

*There are limits to what you owe your grandparents, Becky*, Les had said, but he was wrong. How could there be, when what they gave me was not only their acceptance of my silence but so much more, the minnow in the springhouse guarding the water's purity, spiders spinning webbed words, whip-poor-wills and white owls, woolly worms and snake skins, the sink of a star. All had resonance, meaning. Folklore, yes, but always in one way true, the seamless connection that Hopkins saw: *Each mortal thing does one thing and the same.* What *limits*: that after the morning in the school basement, *word* and *wonder* and *world* could be one.

At the park Carlos has the warning signs posted. I check in with him and then walk downstream to make sure no dead fish are there. As I cross the bridge, Les's thorned words.

*You've been wrong before.*

*Don't think of anything but here and now, only here, only now.* On a maypop vine a saddleback caterpillar clings. *Acharia stimulea.* Oarlike legs, green and brown white-bristled body. Soon it will sleep in its self-spun shroud, winter dreaming as spring's moth-wings slowly sprout. At my feet are snakeroot and sumac, farther on knotweed and skullcap. I whisper each name. Above me birch and beech, red oak and shagbark hickory. In the thicker canopy, stilts of sunlight stalk the ground.

The trail sways closer to the stream. A mane of whitewater falls off a stone shelf, lands loudly. Then the creek curves into shadow. Ferns sleeve both banks green. Water softly licks stone. On a sandbar an otter's tracks. The world's first words ever printed: *I was here.* In Lascaux too: amid that floating menagerie, reed-blown red pigment holds the human hand aloft, oncepresence indelible. Where the otter left the stream, the tail's drag makes an exclamation point. The woods pull back and sunlight surprises the water. Glitters of pyrite. I lift a piece of rock crystal. Time smoothed. What patience to have all edges worn away. As I roll it over my palm, colors gather and spill. I set the stone back and take the loop trail to the meadow, then follow the stream to the park boundary. Across the road I see a DENR van. A resort worker with a black plastic bag gathers dead fish. As he moves upstream, the turkey buzzards flap from branch to branch. Like all *Cathartidae*, voiceless.

I stand in a patch of clover, only then realize I haven't seen a single honeybee. I turn to go back and as I do the meadow withers into dust. Trees melt like candles and the mountains blacken. I lean forward, palms on knees, and take deep steady breaths. I slowly raise my head. The meadow and trees have returned. It is here, and I am here.

But I have seen this world

       a world become

            where wind and water

                        pass

                          past

      unheard

# Twenty-one

It was midafternoon when Jarvis set the kerosene can on my desk.

"It was empty, I assume."

"Empty as a church on Saturday night," Jarvis said as he took off his gloves and sat down. "Think it's the same one he used when he burned his son's house down?"

I lifted the can and looked it over. There was little rust but plenty of dents. Only the red D and E hadn't worn off.

"I don't remember, but it could be."

"It's got to be old enough," Jarvis said.

"My grandfather had one like it, same kind of spout and wood handle." I set the can down. "And it was on Gerald's land, not the resort's?"

"Just barely inside the fence. I nearly tripped over it,"

Jarvis said. "I guess Gerald wanted to make damn sure Tucker knew who did it. I'd say we can put this one in the case-closed file, Sheriff."

"What is it?" Jarvis asked when I didn't respond.

"I don't know," I sighed. "It's just that when I drove up to Gerald's house, he was sitting on his porch drinking coffee like nothing had happened. When I told him why I'd come, he acted like he didn't know what I was talking about. Why do that if two hours earlier you made sure people knew you'd done it?"

"Couldn't it be dementia?"

"That's one answer," I said. "I'll make sure Dr. Washburn checks for signs of that before he's released."

"Or he could be faking that he has it."

"I can't see him faking something like that."

"Why not?"

"His pride," I answered, "but I'm probably just overthinking this thing, putting in too many ifs and buts. Hell, everything points to Gerald having done it."

"Like you've said before, Sheriff, when you hear hoofbeats it's best to assume a horse is coming, not a zebra. What do you want me to do with that kerosene can?"

"Put it in the evidence room."

"Okay," Jarvis said, but he didn't get up. "There's something else I need to talk to you about."

"All right."

"What you've done with the pot dealers. I get that it's the meth doing the serious damage in this county and that's what I'll focus on too, but the way you've done it . . ."

"You mean the payoffs?"

"I'm not judging you," Jarvis said. "I'm just saying."

I waited as he studied the floor a few moments, then met my eyes.

"I'm not going to do that."

"That's your decision, Jarvis," I answered. "You do what's right for you."

"I will," Jarvis said, sounding relieved.

"Anything else?"

"Carly brought in Barry's uniform, so it's clear he's not changing his mind. Should it be me or you who starts looking for a new deputy?"

"You should. He'll be working for you, not me."

Jarvis picked up one glove and set it carefully atop the other, fingers to fingers, thumb over thumb.

"You know, when she pointed at that microwave, I wanted to walk out of that trailer too."

"But you didn't," I said. "I think you and me both realized that Barry wouldn't last very long on this job."

"I guess so, but it's made me think about some things," Jarvis said. "Like three years ago, when the river flooded and they brought in that cadaver dog. I was out there when it found that woman's body."

"I remember. That's something nobody wants to see."

"It wasn't so much seeing her body," Jarvis said. "It was what the handler told me, about how those dogs can last only a few years. She said after they've found enough bodies the dogs get so depressed they can't do the job anymore. Barry's like that, but you and me, we aren't, are we?"

"I guess not."

"But still," Jarvis said. "We have to feel that way at times too, don't we? The only difference is that, unlike those dogs and Barry, we can get past it. I mean, you've felt that way, right? Real sad, and you thought you couldn't deal with it anymore?"

"Once," I said.

# Twenty-two

There are certain odors in a hospital that all the disinfectant in the world can't hide. Sometimes it's blood and pus on a piece of gauze, or a bedsheet stained with urine. It's the smell of suffering. I'd come here when my parents were dying, and I'd come on sheriff business as well, sometimes to the building's lower region where what had brought me slid out on a metal tray. But my strongest memory was the evening I came because of Sarah.

*No one can understand depression unless they've experienced it.* That's what the pamphlet given to me had said, what Dr. Edgar himself told me that day I sat in his office with Sarah. So I was no different from anyone else who hadn't experienced it. Those evenings I stayed at Burrell's Taproom drinking beer, the mornings I left the house without speaking a word, the unreturned phone calls at work, even the outburst the day of the meth raid—all were justified, even inevitable, for *anyone* dealing with something they couldn't understand. I'd told myself that many times.

I checked in at the nursing station and walked down a hall, the white walls and fluorescent lighting reminding me of Trey Yarbrough's pawnshop. But the rooms all had their shadows. I stepped inside Gerald's. The ceiling light was off, the table lamp as well.

Beside the bed, machines blinked and beeped. *He'll be okay this time,* Dr. Washburn had told me in the ER, but added that Gerald should be living nearer the hospital, the same thing C.J. had said two days ago. I stepped closer. The hospital gown made Gerald look infantile. The strangest thought came to me. When a baby was born, was it possible for a parent to imagine that child being this old?

"He's better," a voice said.

Becky rose from a chair in the corner. She went to the bed and placed her palm on Gerald's forehead, then gently smoothed back a few gray hairs.

"We should go to the lobby," she said softly.

There was a coffee urn on a table and Becky poured herself a cup. I thought about getting some as well, but just being here had stirred up enough already for sleep not to come easily. We sat down on the couch. On the wall opposite us, a muted television showed blue water and bright-colored fish. I watched them a few moments.

"I know why Gerald was up there this morning," Becky said.

"I think we all do."

"Gerald told me and it's not what you think," Becky said. "Tucker's secretary called him Tuesday night. She told Gerald that Tucker wanted to meet with him Wednesday morning, just the two of them."

"At the waterfall?"

"Yes. Tucker wanted to straighten out things between them."

"No security up there or anything?" I asked. "Just the two of them?"

"Yes."

"That makes no sense. Gerald's so drugged he could say anything."

"He was clear about that," Becky said. "He told me twice. You can trace the phone call, right?"

"Yes, *if* there was such a phone call. Even if it isn't the drugs, Gerald could still be confused. I told Dr. Washburn to do some cognitive tests before he's released."

"Gerald doesn't have dementia," Becky said, emphatic enough that a nurse looked our way. "I've been around him more than anyone else, and I haven't seen a single sign of it."

"Jarvis found an old Dephas kerosene can next to

Gerald's pasture, right where a path leads up to the water-fall. It's Gerald's, isn't it?"

"Even if it is, that doesn't mean it was used up there."

"The can was empty, Becky."

"He didn't kill those trout, Les," Becky said. "At his house this morning, you saw how he reacted. He didn't know what we were talking about. He was telling the truth and it wasn't dementia."

"Let's hear what Dr. Washburn says. If Gerald is okay mentally, then we can start checking other things. We'll know more about that in the morning."

For a few moments the only sound was a nurse's soft-soled steps. I reached for Becky's hand, unsure if she would let me hold it. She did.

"That comment about you being wrong about people," I said softly. "That was a shitty thing to say. I apologize."

"It's true though," Becky said, "the part about Richard, at least."

For a couple of minutes we didn't speak. On the TV screen a mountain lion had replaced the ocean fish. The locale was out West, maybe the Rockies.

"Tucker could have done this to keep Gerald from going up there," Becky said.

"Go to that much trouble and expense?" I asked. "Think of the risk for Tucker. All that to keep one old man off his property?"

"You think it's not possible?" Becky said stubbornly.

"Look," I answered, trying to keep my voice calm. "It's been a long day for both of us. We need to get some rest. This thing will sort itself out soon enough." I gave Becky's hand a gentle squeeze. "Okay?"

"Okay," Becky said, "but if Gerald gets to go home in the morning, I want to take him. I'll pay the bail money if I need to."

"I'll let Gerald go home if Dr. Washburn says he is all right, and there won't be any bail. But after his high jinks on Monday, he *will* wear an ankle monitor, and if he so much as takes a step off his own property, he's headed to jail."

I got up but Becky didn't.

"Come on, I'll walk out with you."

"I'm going to stay," Becky said.

I freed my hand from hers but resettled it on her shoulder once I stood.

"Tomorrow could be harder than today. You need to get some rest."

"The nurse told me I can sleep on a couch. She said they have a blanket and pillow I can use."

"I'm trying to care for you," I said gently, and realized as soon as I'd spoken that *trying* could be taken two ways. I suddenly realized something else—that day at her mother's house, when Sarah answered *I know you didn't* when I'd told her *I didn't mean it*, she and I may have been speaking of two different things.

"I care about you," I began again. "I'm trying to help you."

Becky raised her hand and set it on mine.

"What Tucker said about the fight, I wish I'd never heard that. Richard changed, and it was for the worse. But I've got to believe people can change for the better. I *have* to, Les."

"I hope they can too," I said.

"You will check about the phone call?"

"If Dr. Washburn says Gerald's okay, I will check it."

When I got back home, I wanted to sleep but too much jangled inside my head. What Becky had said about Gerald loving the trout too much to kill them gave me pause, but I'd known more than one suicide to kill their pets first, as if, like the old Egyptians, they believed the animals would accompany them to the other side.

Then I realized something I should have thought of sooner. A full five-gallon can of kerosene would weigh forty or fifty pounds, and then to haul it up a ridge . . . Gerald was country strong, as people say, but could his heart take the strain?

A horse, not a zebra, I reminded myself. Things almost always *are* what they seem.

But still.

# *Twenty-three*

I sleep a few hours and awake just after midnight. A second blanket is over me, some nurse's kindness. But no sound or smell soothes, all light skystarved. I check on Gerald. Despite the flashing lights, he sleeps soundly, so I take the elevator to the first floor, walk past the parking lot to sit on a concrete bench. Above, night's high tide washup of stars. A car passes near but then there is silence.

*Lord, send my roots rain.*

Hopkins in a moment of wavering faith.

A memory of the Christmas morning two weeks after leaving my grandparents' farm. The tree by the front window tinseled, coiled around it green cords blinking white, a spiked star on the tree's leader, presents underneath. The breakfast of hot cider, ambrosia, and fruit cake. *Everything is exactly the same as last Christmas,* my mother told me. *You are even wearing the same sweater as last year,* she said. *Not a bit of difference,* my father agreed as he handed me my first present. *Can't you at least pretend to act grateful, to at least say thank you,* my father had said.

So I said it.

The trade-off with school and parents from seventh grade on—make good grades, speak if spoken to, and no more counselors and doctors. You can sit in the classroom's back corner, in empty rooms at lunch and at breaks, in your bedroom behind a closed door. But from then until I left home, I'd never been allowed to stay on the farm, for the summer or even a weekend. *If you punish us, we punish you,* my parents had said. The détente of college and after: those visits to that place I could not call *home.* Then the February night of my last year in grad school, my father dead, my mother in a hospital dying.

*You can't know how it felt to watch other parents with their children, to know that we were viewed as failures, parents who had to send you away so others could get you to speak again. You think of us as bad parents, bad people, but can't you understand that after a while, after we did all that we knew to do, that you simply wore us out?*

Vorago of memory threatens. I close my eyes and will myself to a different past day. How many years ago: thirty-one. Thirty-one years ago and a little after midnight.

I would be at the farm, asleep between my grandparents. And when I awoke the next morning, I'd get dressed and eat, then quickly out to the barn. As the morning sun gilds the barn's tin, the warmth softly enfolds me. *I am here and I have never left. I am safe inside the silence of bright wings.*

# PART FOUR

## Twenty-four

My alarm clock was set for seven but when I woke it glowed 5:50. I lay in bed a long while but couldn't go back to sleep, so I made some coffee and sat on the back step. The sky was dark but not silent. East of town geese honked as they followed the river south. It was a far-off, lonely sound, all the more so because it was somewhere in the darkness, like a late-night train whistle or a coyote's howl. I was thinking about the kerosene can, how it surely was the same one Gerald emptied to destroy William's house. Had Gerald thought of that? Maybe, but maybe not. My first year as sheriff I'd asked a woman what she was thinking when she stole a neighbor's Christmas wreath. *I wasn't thinking. I just done it,* she'd answered.

I ate breakfast and lingered over a second cup of coffee. Dr. Washburn would examine Gerald at nine and I planned to be present, especially since I knew Becky would be there. But at eight o'clock my home phone rang and it was Ben Lindsey.

I didn't use the siren but kept the blue light on most of the way, though that was more about driving fast to get to the hospital by nine. I'd made this same trip a year ago to arrest Robin after she'd forged a prescription. She hadn't done prison time but it had cost her parents plenty in lawyers' fees. Now it looked like they might lose the bail money Ben had put up on Tuesday.

He met me at the door, stepped back so I could come in. Martha stood in the doorway that separated the front room and kitchen. She'd been a looker when we were younger, and bearing three children hadn't changed that. Even two years ago, Martha had a face and figure most women in their thirties would envy. No longer. Now she seemed melted into a pale shapelessness, though a darker swelling lay under her eyes, as if the grief had pooled there. I sat down on the couch, though no one had invited me to.

"I told him not to bail her out," Martha said, then turned to Ben. "I told you and you done it anyway."

"What did she take?" I asked.

"My wedding ring," Martha answered, "that and what money Ben had in his billfold and me in my purse. And a gold pocket watch Ben's daddy gave him."

"Anything else?"

"What else is there?" Martha hissed through clenched teeth. "She's done used up all our savings on lawyers and bondsmen and the rehab center. She's took everything but that baby sleeping in the back room, leaving her for us to raise."

"Martha," Ben said quietly.

"I'll not raise it," Martha said, her voice louder, more bitter. "There's no telling what's wrong with it after breathing that meth. Social services can give that baby to any that's willing to take it."

"You know where Robin might have gone?" I asked.

"Charlotte maybe," Ben said. "That's where she went the other time."

"Then she come back here when even the trash she lived with down there wouldn't have her," Martha said, glaring at me now. "I know what busybodies like Bobbi Moffitt are saying about us in town and it's a lie. We raised two children that don't do drugs or drink. They both hold down jobs and never had the least trouble with the law. If we were such bad parents, how was it that they turned out good?"

Martha began crying, but when Ben went to hold her she slapped his arm away.

"Leave me be," she shouted, and as she did a baby's cry came from a back room. "I ain't deserved this, and I'd say it to God himself. I'd say it to His face and I'd dare him to claim otherwise."

"I'm going to see about the baby," Ben said.

Martha wiped her eyes, then followed.

I heard a door open, then close. The baby quit crying. I looked around the room. When I'd been here last year, the fireplace mantel was crowded with family photographs, but now there were pictures of only the two older children, or of the family before Robin had been born. When I stepped closer to the mantel, I smelled smoke.

Ben came back into the room, alone. My cell phone buzzed but I left it in my pocket.

"Sorry you had to witness this, Les. It's just been hard, on all of us." Ben took a slip of paper from his shirt pocket. "Here's a list of what's missing."

"If you hear from Robin, let me know," I said as I took the paper. "I'll tell Trey Yarbrough to look out for the pocket watch and ring, just in case she's still around."

We walked out to the porch.

"I guess you've still got a photo of her," Ben said.

"We do."

"The ones we had of her, Martha burned before you came. Every one of them. I didn't stop her. I wanted to," he said. "I wanted to," he said again, more softly.

"I'd better be on my way," I said.

It felt wrong to offer a handshake but Ben reached

out to me, not to take my hand but to grasp my forearm.

"You've seen some folks that were able to get off this meth, ain't you? I mean, there's some."

"Yes," I answered as Ben released my arm. "There's some."

It was almost nine, so when I got back in the patrol car I called Jarvis, told him that he'd need to take an ankle monitor to the hospital in case Gerald got discharged.

"If that's the way you want to handle this," Jarvis said, disapproval in his tone.

Like the pot bribes, Jarvis was letting me know things would be different with him in charge. That was a good thing, but he would learn in time that a sheriff could bend the law for no other reason than what was law and what was right sometimes differed.

Ben remained on the porch as I drove off. Not wanting to go inside, or maybe waiting for Robin to show up, bring back what she'd taken and make everything all right. One story my grandfather told me about his days as a sandhog had seemed a tall tale, even to a kid, but later I'd found out it was true. In the years before electricity, what light burned inside the underwater caissons came from candles. At the greatest depths, the pressure was such that the candles wouldn't blow out. The flame would sail off the wick, ricochet around the walls, then resettle on the wick. What my grandfather hadn't told me was that sometimes cables broke and a man would be trapped down there. He'd know the candle was burning up oxygen, and he'd know the flame would not go out, but he'd keep blowing anyway, even with his last breaths, still hoping against hope that, somehow, it might.

# Twenty-five

"They told me if I wanted to stay for lunch I could," Gerald snorts as we leave the hospital. "Likely as not they'd have laid another slab of green Jell-O on my plate. The only thing good I swallowed the whole time was that spring water you brung me."

"At least Dr. Washburn released you early."

"Not before he gave me a bunch of advice I didn't ask for," Gerald said.

"You need to listen to what he tells you."

"Seems like that's all people do anymore," Gerald grumbles, "tell me what I can or can't do."

"If you're real hungry," I say as I turn onto Main Street, "we can stop at Greene's Café."

"No, I want to go home and fix a real breakfast," Gerald says. "Anyway, I'm in no mood to be around folks. I had a full portion of that yesterday. And now this thing on my ankle, like I'm a damn dog or something."

"At least you'll be home," I say.

Outside town, a roadside apple stand has opened. Red delicious and Granny Smiths brim the latticed baskets. Like the half-mown hay field across the road, a harbinger of mornings when firm ground crackles and white breaths precede, trees start unblending and the leafers appear. Though a difference these last few years. Once out of their vehicles, the tourists raise cameras or cell phones, as if unable to see without them. I think of what Richard said, *They won't even know they are in the world.*

When the resort comes in sight, Gerald tenses. Beside the stream is a white truck with a steel tank and an aerator, which means DENR's declared the water safe. Two men lift sopping dip nets of rainbow trout. They hold the mesh bottoms, twist the long handles. Silvery scales catch sunlight. Bright as fresh-struck coins, trout spill and splash.

"I didn't kill them fish," Gerald says as we pull into his driveway. "It was Tucker's doing that I was even up there."

"Les is going to check the phone call," I say.

I give Gerald his key and he unlocks the door.

"I know what this is about," Gerald says once we're

inside. "Tucker figured to get me back by blaming them dead fish on me."

Gerald says it loud, like he's talking to the house, not me.

"If you get too upset, you'll be in the hospital again."

"But that's the what-for of him doing it," Gerald says. "Ain't it?"

"I don't know," I answer. "You need to eat. If you make the coffee, I'll cook."

I set the skillet on the stove, get butter and eggs from the refrigerator while Gerald fills the pot with water, places the basket inside, and scoops in the grounds. Soon the familiar soothes. We sit down and Gerald eats as I sip coffee.

My cell phone buzzes and Les's number comes up. I step out in the yard to answer.

"Are you with Gerald?" Les asks.

"Yes, but he can't hear me. Have you talked to Dr. Washburn?"

"I just did."

"And he said Gerald's mind is fine."

"A *cursory* exam showed no dementia," Les says. "To be positive he'll have to do more tests."

"Gerald's mind is clear," I say, "and he's certain about that phone call from the resort. It was between seven and nine on Tuesday night. Have you checked?"

"No."

"But you will?"

"Yes."

"Do you want to talk to Gerald about the telephone call?"

"Let's be sure there was a call first," Les says. "Then we'll go from there."

"How long will it take to know?"

"It depends. Probably a few hours."

"But you'll call me as soon as you know?"

"Yes, Becky, but you've got to be patient."

"I know."

"What about Gerald?" Les asks. "He's not acting like he might throw another tantrum, is he?"

"No."

"Well, he best stay that way."

"Does he have to wear the ankle bracelet? It's humiliating for him."

"It's that or a jail cell," Les says.

I text Carlos that I'll be at the park in fifteen minutes. As I put up the cell phone, Gerald comes out on the porch with our coffee mugs.

"Let's have a look at the garden," he says.

I follow him into the corn patch. Passing between rows, my fingertips linger on the shucks, a ripple feel like a comb's teeth. *We will harvest these together*, I tell myself. *We will.*

"Look how beardy them tassels are," Gerald says. "This corn's soon to be ready."

We check the tomatoes last, what few left plump and blushing. Gerald picks one, polishes it with his shirttail, and sets it on the porch. He comes back and kneels to pull up some weeds.

"I've got to go to work but I'll come back at noon," I say. "You'll be okay till then, won't you?"

Gerald grabs another hank of weeds and jerks hard enough that ground comes with them.

"Yeah, I'll be okay," Gerald says, hurling the clump into the side yard.

"This will be over soon, I promise."

"Not soon enough," Gerald says.

"Pick us out one more tomato," I say. "I'll make us sandwiches for lunch."

Gerald stands and brushes the dirt off his overalls.

"All right," he says, but his voice softens. "Thanks for coming to get me. I know I'm acting ornery, but what's happened has got me all out of sorts."

"I know," I say. "Call if you need anything before I get back."

As I drive to the park, I see that a sweet gum's leaves have begun to turn. I think not of fall's beginning but its end, remembering a snowy afternoon on my grandparents' farm, my last week there. Booted and bundled, I'd walked beneath branches forked like stalled lightning. Woods surrounded me as soft flakes fell. In every direction the silence of so much: *Promise not to speak, children, don't say a single word. Be completely silent.* There in those woods I did so. Completely still as my boots dusted white and the woods darkened. Then came a tap on my left shoulder, the flutter of wings settling. The blessing of that moment. The cardinal rose, disappeared into deeper woods.

# Twenty-six

"He's yet got a mouth on him," Hubert McClure, the first shift guard, said. "You'd think after two days he'd start to wind down."

Rodney Greer sat on the cot, dressed in his orange county issue, barefoot, with arms folded tight across his stomach. Greer wasn't shaking as bad as the first day, but with his scabby arms and blistered lips he still looked like someone who'd spent a week in a lifeboat. Despite Greer's big talk about lawyers, no one had even made his bail.

"It ain't right I'm still here and her out," he whined. "All the stuff in my trailer, that whore brought it with her. I don't know nothing about mixing chemicals. Just look at my high school report card. I failed science two years straight. And that baby, I told her it needed to be took better care of. That's the God's truth, Sheriff. Bring me in a Bible. I'll swear on it."

"Greer, can you speak any language other than bullshit?" Hubert said.

"You doubting my faith?"

"He's something, ain't he?" Hubert said to me. "They ought to run this scoundrel for governor. He's got all the makings."

Hubert grinned, revealing a gold front tooth, a replacement for a real one lost while a teen playing anejodi. He was a decade older than me, but his hair had the same blue-black sheen as twenty years back when he took the job. It was the hair, more than anything else, that told you Scots-Irish was only a quarter of his ancestry.

I stepped closer to the bars that separated Rodney Greer and me.

"Where would Robin Lindsey go if she wanted to hide?" I asked.

Greer gave a weak smile.

"Skipped bail, didn't she?"

"Where would she go?" I asked again.

"Charlotte, maybe," Greer said. "Every time she threatened to take off, it was to there."

"Where in Charlotte?"

"I don't know. She had friends there but I never met them."

"What about around here?"

"Just her parents' house," Greer said. "She and Cissy Hawkins were big buddies before Cissy OD'd."

"Anyone else?"

Greer shook his head. I stepped away from the bars, nodded toward a man snoring in the other cell.

"Who's that?"

"Some guy from South Carolina named Singleton."

"What's his story?"

"Clint brought him in last night," Hubert said, and grinned. "The fool was pissing on a fire hydrant at the rec center. Clint said he wasn't sure if he should bring him here or take him to the pound."

I went back upstairs. Jarvis was checking out a break-in on Tillis Pond Road, another bad meth area, so Ruby and I were the only ones around.

"Anything else come in?" I asked her.

"That hiker called again."

"I'll go out there," I said, "but I need to phone a couple of folks first."

I called Rance Foster, my Bell South contact, and gave him the date and time to check.

"Give me an hour," Rance said.

I called the Charlotte Police Department about Robin Lindsey in case she'd gotten picked up for something there, but they didn't have anything. I thought about Martha burning the photographs. If you didn't know the family, you'd look at the mantel and not know Robin existed. During our evening of wine and openness last May, I'd asked Becky about her childhood before the shooting. "After" the morning of the shooting, she'd told me, she couldn't remember any "before." When she'd been brought home, she'd gone into her bedroom and thought, *Whose room is this?* She'd opened the closet and all of the drawers, touching each object, thinking that once everything had been touched, she'd remember whose past it had been. "I did that for days," Becky had said, "but it never worked, so I quit trying."

I heard Jarvis talking to Ruby about the break-in, so I called him into my office.

"What'd they take?" I asked as he sat down.

"A television and a generator were the main things, but get this," Jarvis said. "They stole a frigging Waterpik."

"That is pretty funny. Dental hygiene has never been much of a priority with these folks."

"I expect we have similar ideas about who did it."

"In that part of the county, I'd say someone named Campbell, Pinson, or Merck. I'd put Peeler in there too except I doubt he's got enough fingers left from that last explosion to steal anything. Darby Ramsey's always a possibility, but he's so lazy I doubt he'd drive that far."

"I was thinking Pinson."

"That's not a bad place to start," I said. "You called Trey Yarbrough yet?"

"No, but I will."

"Mention what Robin Lindsey stole too," I said, handing Jarvis Ben's list. "I doubt she's still in the county, but you never know. How about Gerald, did he give you any trouble?"

"He didn't much like me putting that ankle monitor on him."

"I'm sure he didn't."

"Dr. Washburn told me Gerald's heart is in bad shape," Jarvis said, "but that he's okay cognitively."

"Dr. Washburn told me the same."

"So I guess it comes down to him being a better liar than we'd have reckoned," Jarvis said. "Or he didn't do it. You still think there's a chance of that?"

"There's one last thing I want to confirm, about a telephone call, and it ought to settle that question once and for all."

"Soon?"

"Within the hour," I said, and got up from my chair. "I'm going to go have a look at that National Forest campsite."

"I'll be glad to go."

"No," I answered. "I'll do it."

So maybe for the last time as sheriff I headed toward

Mist Creek Valley, not all the way but enough to stir up memories. I turned on the radio, a country oldies station. Johnny Cash sang of hard times chopping cotton in Arkansas. There was a hurt in Cash's voice that all the fame and riches he'd acquired had never healed. Cash's brother died when they were both children, and somehow Cash had been made to feel responsible. I thought of my uncle and Daddy and what my grandfather had done to them. *The worst thing was the sound of that belt being jerked through his pants' loops,* my uncle had told me after Daddy died. *A hissing sound, like it was a snake coiled around him and he'd grabbed it by the tail and was whipping it to death, the only difference being a snake would have been dead long before he was through with your daddy and me.*

I passed the bullet-pocked NATIONAL FOREST sign and drove the mile up an old logging road to a clearing with campsites and a parking area. No vehicles today, but buzzards flapped upward as I got out. My first thought was a drug deal gone bad or an OD, but instead, a few yards into the woods was a dog's carcass, dumped there by someone too sorry to bury it. I picked up a plastic Mountain Dew bottle and sniffed. Meth. I kicked around in the broom sedge, some of it matted by tires, some standing, and found an empty Sudafed packet, a couple of vials, one needle and a syringe, which I picked up by its plunger and set on the car hood. I got a bag and placed the needle and syringe in it. My cell phone buzzed.

"Here's your info," Rance said. "No local calls in or out between six and midnight. Two 800 numbers, which means telemarketers, at 7:05, 7:48. At 8:10, a fifty-eight second call from a Tennessee number."

"But the 800 calls couldn't be from Tucker's resort?"

"Those calls were from New York and Atlanta."

"And the other call," I asked. "You're certain it's from Tennessee?"

"It was from a cell phone so you'd have to get the owner's name from Verizon, but it was a 323 area code."

"Okay," I said. "Thanks."

"I know someone who can check that Tennessee number," Rance said, "though of course it could be some kind of telemarketer too. They're getting sneakier all the time."

"Give me the number and I'll try it," I said and hung up.

So Gerald had lied, not just to me and to C.J. but to Becky as well.

For a few moments I listened. A squirrel chattered deeper in the woods. Closer, a small creek murmured. Nature brought out the best in humans, Becky said, but here, as deep into nature as you could get in this county, I saw just the opposite. I kicked around a bit more, turned up a green Bic lighter, a pill bottle cap, more empty foil packets, drink tabs, and cigarette butts.

It was only as I walked back to the car that I noticed the flower. I stepped closer to confirm the green basal leaves beneath the lavender bloom. *Blazing star.* I'd gone with Becky to see some like it near Boone last September. So rare in North Carolina they were classified as endangered, Becky had told me. But here was one. I looked around and found five more.

I got back in the patrol car but I didn't start the engine. I sat for a few minutes. Then I drove toward town, but when I got to Poplar Road I turned and drove a half mile, parked in front of a house that hadn't been occupied for eight years. Kudzu vines smothered one side. Part of the tin roof lay among the vines, glinting in the early afternoon sun. I went up the creaking steps. On the porch lay tatters of the yellow police tape we'd put up after the raid. The door was open. I stepped inside. Some broken glass and dishes, a couch moldering in a corner, scattered sections of old newspaper.

He had not threatened me. He hadn't said a word, just raised the pistol and pointed it at my face. *That gun was aimed at you a full minute*, Jarvis told me later. Your life flashes before you, I'd always heard, but it hadn't for me. It was as if I stood in the corner, not so much observing as performing a methodical self-autopsy, not of my body but of my life. I had not been frightened. Instead, I'd felt a calm clarity. Everything inside me, including my heart, seemed suspended, except for one thought: *What will you miss?* A full minute and I'd had no answer. Then the gun was lowered, and I slowly, reluctantly, came back into myself. Cuffs clicked and we went out the door.

Now, eight years later, I stood in the same room and asked myself that same question.

I stepped back onto the porch and called the Tennessee cell phone number. No one answered, and there was no voice mail set up. I punched in Rance's number.

"How about getting your buddy to check that Verizon number?" I asked him. "I just called it but didn't get an answer."

"Sure," Rance said. "I'm not sure how long it will take though."

"That's okay."

Then I called Ruby on the radio and told her I was going to see Harold Tucker.

# Twenty-seven

Farm Pond
*Worn gapped boards balance on stilts,*
*walk toward the pond's deep end.*
*A green smell simmers shallows,*
*where tadpoles flow like black tears.*
*Minnows lengthen their shadows.*
*Something unseen stirs the reeds.*

Carp
*Let it live where nothing else can,*
*downstream from poison pours,*
*beneath surface-skin rainbows of oil,*
*let it graze silt-stir, stomach offal,*
*let its survival never absolve us.*

*Snake Doctor*
*Minister whose idling cross-shadow blesses*
*even before wings still and the virid touch*

I write

*soothes the talon-rake of owl and hawk.*

I rewrite the line to balance the consonants.

*heals the talon-rake of hawk and eagle.*

The school bus arrives. I put the notebook back in my office and lead them downstream to the small waterfall where I recite

*A wind-puff bonnet of fawn-froth*
*Turns and twindles over the broth.*

You don't have to understand the words, I tell them. Just let the sounds enter you, the same as everything else you see and smell and touch today.

I show them deer and beaver tracks, some wildflowers and insects, before we walk up to the meadow where we all sit down. No breeze: early fall's stillness like a carousel paused. The children feel it too, speak in whispers.

*What does silence look like?*

I ask them to think about an answer. As they do, several children tilt their heads to one side, listening.

"It looks like air," a child says.

"What else does it look like?" I ask.

"It looks like night, but not scary."

"It looks like the wind when the wind's not blowing."

"What about you, Ms. Douglas?" a child asks the teacher.

"Hmmm," she says. "How about that it looks like paper that hasn't been written on."

"Plain paper with no lines," a child says.

"Yes," the teacher agrees. "No lines."

"And what about you?" a child asks me.

"Like stars resting on a calm pond," I answer.

Several small heads nod.

"It's time for us to go," the teacher says, and we stand up, brush bits of ground off our clothes. We are almost to the bus when a child who hasn't spoken turns to me.

"I know what silence looks like," she says.

"What?" I ask.

"It looks like someone asleep," the child says.

"Yes," I tell the child as she boards the bus. "It does."

It does, it did:

They had made us go. A way to help all the children heal, they said. *The undertaker did the best he could*, a gray-haired woman whispered as my parents and I entered. Sad music in the walls of a large white room. Flowers, fresh but dead, smothering a long gray box. Grown-up tears, large hands I was made to shake. *We know you will miss your teacher. She is over there. Don't you want to tell her good-bye? All the other children have. Don't be frightened, child, she looks like she's asleep.* Hands urged me closer to the gray box but I tried to pull free. Mr. Kestner, the principal, kneeled beside me. *Don't you think she'd want you to tell her good-bye?* I shook my head, because what Ms. Abernathy had wanted from us was silence.

## Twenty-eight

On that late-summer morning, we'd been spraying conditioner on the hay baler's belts, C.J. on the left, me on the right. It was an old Vemeer, the rollers no more than an inch apart and its metal tines grabbing whatever they touched. We wore long-sleeved flannel shirts so the bales wouldn't chafe our arms. I let a sleeve get too close and a tine grabbed the cloth and jerked my arm toward the rollers. There are times when a single second can stretch like taffy and that happened when the baler snatched my shirtsleeve. I saw my sleeve and the button on my cuff and my hand and I saw where my sleeve and cuff and hand were about to go. C.J. grabbed my wrist just before my flesh touched the spinning rollers. Another few inches and both our arms would have been torn off. The tines missed my hand but not C.J.'s. Scars he yet bore. I'd never thanked him for what he'd done, never even acknowledged to him or anyone else that it was my fault. I'd been silent when the doctor scolded C.J. for being careless, silent when his great-uncle drove us to the hospital. *He can say what happened easy as I can,* I'd told myself. *It's his choice to take the blame.*

I went up the lodge's porch steps and into the lobby. It was an impressive room, corbeled creek-rock fireplace, exposed beams on the ceiling. The wormy chestnut paneling held the smell of wood smoke. Two huge trout, one a brown, one a rainbow, made frozen leaps above the receptionist's desk. I sat down and waited, thinking about C.J. Classmates who'd bullied him called C.J. a coward when he hadn't fought back, but he'd been brave and selfless when he'd risked himself to save me. *In the very core of my being, who am I?* C.J. had answered the question that day on his uncle's farm. There were people who live their whole lives never knowing the answer. Others do, and, whether with pride or shame, they lived with that knowledge.

"You can go in now," the receptionist said. "It's the last room on the right."

Tucker didn't stand when I entered, simply nodded at the armchair opposite his desk. On the wall was a framed photograph of the resort staff, C.J. among them.

"So why this visit, Sheriff?"

"I wanted to talk to you about C.J."

"What about him?"

"I don't think he should lose his job. Whatever's happened was more my fault than his. I knew Gerald might come over here and I should have made sure that he didn't. Even more so with the fish kill. If Gerald's responsible, that's on me too. I could have locked him up for threats, like you said."

I paused to let Tucker respond but he didn't. Except for a slight frown, his face was expressionless.

"Look, Mr. Tucker," I continued, "even if C.J. didn't handle things perfectly, he's done well for you otherwise. You know how hard he worked to get where he is. You know how he grew up too. I mean, even if you blame this whole mess on him, it's still just one mistake."

"I don't have to justify my employment decisions to you or anyone else, Sheriff."

"I know you don't, Mr. Tucker, but C.J.'s been working for you so long. He can rub people wrong sometimes, but he's as decent a man as I know. Loyalty's very important to you. I've heard you say that more than once."

"You don't think I know these things?" Tucker said, but not harshly.

"I do. All I'm doing is reminding you of what to weigh against one mistake."

"But it wasn't just one mistake and loyalty cuts both

ways," Tucker answered. "When he came here, C.J. had us change some policies. We allowed the locals to pick blackberries, gather mistletoe, that kind of thing, even when some clients complained about them being on the property. Good public relations and something we owed the community, C.J. said, and I went along with it. But this April a poacher pretty much cleaned out the creek between here and the waterfall. I'm talking about fifty to sixty trout, and a lot of them our trophy fish. The smaller ones the bastard caught, he threw on the bank to rot beside his empty corn cans and cigarette butts."

"I never heard about that," I said.

"What could you have done about it if you had?" Tucker asked. "It's not like those trout would show up at a pawnshop. But you know as well as I do that it had to be a local and he ruined it for everybody else. I bought extra security cameras and changed our policy. You've seen the signs. Hell, how can you *not* see them when we've got them posted every twenty yards, and every one makes clear we *will* prosecute. Gerald went up there in June and we got him on camera. Did you know that?"

"C.J. told me Monday."

"Well," Tucker said. "Did C.J. also tell you he lied so I wouldn't find out?"

"No."

"He told my security people that he'd report Gerald

being up there to me and then he told them he had and that it was taken care of. But C.J. didn't report it to me. I didn't find out until this Monday when Gerald came and threatened me. Security pulled up C.J.'s e-mails to prove he'd lied."

"Because C.J. didn't want Gerald prosecuted," I said. "That's the only reason he did it."

"I don't know why. What I do know is that he lied to three of my employees. He lied to me too, with his actions if not his words. And now you've seen the consequences of his lying. It was out there in the creek. You're right about me, Sheriff, loyalty is important, and loyalty and honesty are inseparable. My workers know that, and every time one of them has broken that trust they've been fired. No exceptions, and there never will be. C.J. *has* done good work for me though and I'll do what I can for him. I'll write job recommendations and I'll say only positive things. I'll blame the economy for his being let go. But he's never going to work here again."

I waited a few moments. As with the tone in his voice, nothing in Tucker's face gave hope he'd change his mind.

"C.J.'s been a friend of mine since we were teenagers," I said. "You know that."

"Yes," Tucker said.

"How did he take it when you fired him?"

"Not very well. He tried to get me to change my mind.

He brought up his sons, told me how hard he'd worked to give them a good life and how if I fired him they'd not have that. I told him I was sorry but he'd made a choice and had to live with the consequences. Then he left."

"Was he angry?"

"Not at me," Tucker said. "He was mad at himself, and at Gerald, of course. He knew I was in the right."

Tucker had told me more than he'd intended. He grimaced and turned his attention to a spreadsheet on his desk.

"Go on about your business, Sheriff," Tucker said, "and I'll go about mine."

When I went back outside, a fisherman was in the creek, his rod curved and throbbing. Then he dipped his net and raised it, in the mesh a foot-long rainbow. He removed the hook and gently lowered the trout to the water, opened his hand and the fish slipped free. Instead of getting back in my car, I walked across the road and tried to spot Becky. I needed to talk to her but didn't see her in the meadow or near the bridge.

My phone buzzed.

"I got your Verizon info," Rance said, "and I've got a feeling you'll find it pretty damn interesting."

"Okay," I said. "Tell me."

"A guy named Levon Carlson bought the phone in Knoxville last January. I figured to save you a bit of time so checked ole Levon out myself. If you're wanting to lock him up, you're too late."

"How's that?"

"Levon is in prison."

"*Prison?*"

"That's right, prison."

"Where?"

"Over in Tennessee at Roan Mountain. He's been locked up for three months. Got busted in Knoxville for dealing drugs."

"And the phone hasn't been confiscated?"

"Hey, that's your area of expertise," Rance said. "All I know is it's his phone that made the call you asked about."

"Thanks," I said, and hung up.

*What the hell is going on?* I thought. Gerald claimed the call was from a woman, yet a woman's voice could be faked. But why would a convict in Tennessee call Gerald? Carlson sure as hell wasn't the one who'd been up there poisoning the trout. A wrong number was still possible. Or maybe Carlson was some distant relative, who, like Darby, wanted something, probably money. Or some pal of Darby's looking for him, and figured his uncle would know.

Or someone had used Carlson to set up Gerald.

But if that was it, whoever asked Carlson to call would surely want any evidence destroyed, meaning the phone would already be broken apart and flushed into the prison's sewer system. Though if that was true, why would it still ring only a couple of hours ago? A call to the prison would give me an answer, but before that I decided to look at the security video again.

"I need to get permission from Mr. Tucker first," Randall Cobb told me.

"I understand."

"Mr. Tucker didn't sound happy about it," Randall said when he hung up, "but he said okay."

I studied the video of Gerald coming up, then had Randall show Gerald going back down. Even though I couldn't see his hands, I saw enough.

"What is it?" Randall asked.

"Look how level his shoulders are, coming and going. If he was carrying a can that weighed forty to fifty pounds, surely one shoulder would be lower, especially after carrying it a quarter-mile up a ridge."

"He's a stout man," Randall said.

"I know, but still. Do a lot of people here know where the cameras are?"

"Of course. Our job's easier if they aren't tripping them all the time."

"I understand," I said.

---

When I came out of the security office, Tucker waited on the lodge's porch.

"Why did you need to see that video again?"

"To be certain that someone other than Gerald poisoned those trout."

"Someone other than Gerald," Tucker said, "and who in the hell might that be?"

"One of your workers."

"It wasn't a goddamn accident, Sheriff. I've already gone over this with DENR. My men would have reported it to me. Like I told you fifteen minutes ago, I don't abide anyone who's not honest around here."

"I'm not saying it was an accident. What if one of them had a grudge against you? Or some locals like that poacher. They wouldn't like those WE PROSECUTE signs."

"Someone did have a grudge against me, Sheriff, and his name is Gerald Blackwelder."

*Go ahead and say it,* I thought, because Tucker was already so royally pissed that I didn't have much to lose.

"Or a worker might have thought he was helping you and the resort get rid of a problem."

Tucker's mouth opened wide enough to show the gold crowns in his back teeth. Then a huffing sound, as if dislodging something in his throat.

"My God," he said, as if marveling at his own words. "You think I did this."

"I'm not accusing," I said, "but—"

"Get off my property," Tucker said. "And if you *ever* come back up here you'd better be hiring a goddamn good lawyer, because I've got three and they'll be on you like a pack of pit bulls."

# Twenty-nine

I drove straight to the courthouse and dialed Roan Mountain prison. After a few transfers, I got Carlson's wing. You had to be diplomatic in these matters, so I mentioned the former warden, a guy I'd met a few times. Joseph, the tier guard, had worked for him and liked him, which was all good for me. When I asked if they'd confiscated a cell phone from a prisoner named Levon Carlson, Joseph said no.

"Tell you what," he said. "I ought to get my superior's okay on this, but hell, I'll have one of my men check. If that phone's in there, even if it's up Carlson's ass, we'll know."

"And if you don't mind, could you tell the guard not to mention what he's looking for?"

"He can say he's searching for contraband."

Joseph asked for my office number and said he'd call back.

"Better that way," he said. "Just so I confirm who you say you are."

"Thanks," I said, and gave my number.

I didn't have to wait long for the call back.

"It's not in his cell, or on him, or in him," Joseph said. "The guard checked every cell on Carlson's tier. No phone."

"I'd still like to talk to Carlson," I said. "Could you let me, by phone?"

"I can't without the warden or his assistant's okay. They've gone to Nashville on state business and won't be back before five."

"It's important."

"I understand, but keeping my job is important too," Joseph said. "I can get it set up in the morning."

"What's the earliest?"

"Nine or so. When I find out, I'll call and let you know."

I gave him my cell phone number and thanked him. I called Dr. Washburn and then met with Jarvis. I got him up to speed on the phone call and what I'd seen on the video.

"I talked to Dr. Washburn," I said. "He doubted Gerald's heart could stand that kind of strain."

"This horse is getting some stripes on it," Jarvis said, "but still, who else would do it?"

"An employee, or former employee, someone who wants to get back at Tucker but not take the blame."

"C.J. Gant would fill that bill," Jarvis said. "He wouldn't mind getting Gerald into trouble either."

That notion was like a scratched match that flares up a moment, but then doesn't catch.

"No, C.J. couldn't do this, even if he was angry enough to."

"Why not?" Jarvis asked.

"Because of his sons. He grew up knowing what it's like to be humiliated by your father. He'd not risk the same for his boys."

"What about someone getting back at Tucker *because* he fired C.J.?"

That was something I'd not thought of. Far-fetched but everything seemed far-fetched now.

"Of course it could be something besides a grudge," I said, "something we haven't even considered."

"What about Darby Ramsey?" Jarvis asked.

"How so?"

"If Gerald got put in prison or declared senile he could do what he liked with the farm, right?"

"No, Darby doesn't have power of attorney," I said. "He knows the only way he gets the farm is when Gerald's dead."

"So it can still be Gerald."

"Yes, it can," I said, "but if my chat with Levon Carlson doesn't settle this, we'll get a list of current and former employees. That will give Tucker something else to be pissed off at me about. I can find out who worked closest with C.J. and I'll have a visit with Darby too. He may be so drug-addled he's forgotten what has to happen for him to get his inheritance."

# *Thirty*

As evening's last light recedes, a silver birch glows like a tuning fork struck. I leave the bike at the station and cross the meadow. I need to feel the earth solid. The air is cool, not cold, but Gerald is building a fire. As always, one of the hearth logs is apple wood. Because its colors make a fire pretty, Gerald says. He places kindling and newspaper as attentively as he might tie a trout fly, then strikes a match. Beneath the andirons the red-tipped wood spore blossoms. Fire streams around kindling, thickens and pools, swirls upward as sparks crackle, splash slowly onto the hearthstone. The apple wood sprouts feathers of redyellowgreen, as if the lost parrot has phoenixed among the flames. Gerald's palms open as if to bless the fire, or maybe it's to have the fire bless him. How many thousands of years that gesture, its promise of light, and heat, and soon-rest summoned.

I make sandwiches and Gerald cuts wedges from a cantaloupe. He fills two glasses with spring water and we eat in silence until Gerald sets his napkin on his plate.

"Want coffee?" Gerald asks.

"No, but thank you."

Gerald pours his coffee and sits back down. The room is already too warm, so Gerald adds no more wood.

"People believe I dumped that poison?" he says, staring at the faltering fire. "Don't they?"

"Maybe some do."

"There ain't no 'maybe' if I'm wearing this damn ankle monitor. Wasn't no maybe in the sheriff coming here soon as it happened, like I was the only one who could of done it." Gerald pauses. "You come with him. I guess you figured I done it too."

"That's not true," I say.

"Then why?"

"I was trying to help you, so was Les."

"By arresting me, then having this damn dog collar put on me?"

"Les didn't have to let you come home, Gerald. He could have put you in jail."

"So he claims," Gerald mutters.

I hesitate, then in little more than a whisper, "Why didn't you tell me C.J. Gant warned you about going up there? If you'd have let me know, maybe none of this would have happened."

"He said not to tell anyone he come by," Gerald answers, not meeting my eyes. "Said he'd get in trouble if anybody found out."

"But you could have told me. You know I would have kept it between us."

"He asked me not to tell anyone and that's what I done."

"Then why did you go back up there, Gerald, when he asked you not to?"

Gerald tightens his fist, then slams it against the chair arm. He stands up, grabs the biggest log from the wood box, and hurls it two-handed into the fireplace. Sparks flurry out and expire.

"Because it was my right, dammit!" Gerald shouts. "When Tucker's folks wandered onto my land I said never a cross word to him or them. I gave them a ride back if they asked me, and took none of the money offered for doing it. I didn't of a sudden say, *I think I'll put the law on you today*. When I went over there, maybe I talked too rough, but those guards had no right to treat me like that. What if I *was* the one that killed them fish? I'd of been in my rights to do it after the way they treated me. Maybe I'll go and dump more poison in that creek, give Tucker real cause to claim I did it."

"Please, Gerald," I say, stepping closer, reaching out my hand to hold his arm, steady both of us, "your heart."

"You nor no one else knows a thing about my heart!" Gerald shouts, jerking my hand away. "Agnes, good a woman as she was, said to me when I burned William's house down, 'You don't know how to grieve, Gerald. All you done is make it about your ownself, not our boy. You've caused folks to come out here and watch that house burn, made a spectacle of your own son's death.' She said that to me, them very words. Later she made claim she didn't mean it, that she was deep in her own black thoughts that day, but Agnes couldn't have said it if she hadn't thought it first."

Gerald cries now. He clenches his big right hand and pounds it once against his chest.

"My heart," he sobs, "nobody but me knows what's alone in my heart."

"Your nitro pills," I say. "Where are they?"

Gerald waves me away, wipes his eyes with a sleeve.

"Do you need them?" I plead, crying now too. "Please, Gerald, tell me."

Gerald steps close to the fireboard, places a hand on it to steady himself. His head is down and he wipes his eyes again.

"You don't need them?"

He doesn't speak or look at me, but shakes his head, does so again when I ask if he's sure he's okay. Then, for a few minutes, only the sound of the expiring fire.

I pull a Kleenex from my pocket and wipe my eyes. I take the plates and glasses to the sink and wash them. Gerald still stands before the hearth but his hand has shifted so that the fingers touch the glass covering the photograph of him and his wife and son.

"I need to go," I tell him, but he doesn't respond.

Few stars glint, but the moon is out, hooped and pale enough to show its craters. I could see better walking up the road, but I enter the meadow, let moonlight and the creek's pebbly rhythms lead me to the station.

*Nobody but me knows what's alone in my heart.*

I get my bike and ride to my cabin, gather my sleeping bag, trail mix, flashlight, and water bottle. A breeze awakens the wind chimes as I step back outside. I listen for a few moments, then ride up the Parkway to a campsite. I put my sleeping bag down and get in. After a while the breeze thickens. Around the moon gray clouds ghost.

# PART FIVE

# *Thirty-one*

*You go that far deep and dark down,* my grandfather once said about being in the caisson, *it makes you love these mountains all the more.* I thought of him saying that as I drove to the courthouse on Friday morning. But I knew that, unlike my grandfather, C.J. was wishing he'd never come back. Last night, I'd almost picked up the phone to call and see if I could do anything to help him or his family. But I'd decided to wait until I talked to Levon Carlson. If someone else had poisoned the creek, I still hoped Tucker might reconsider firing C.J.

"What's got you here so bright and early?" Ruby asked when I came into the office.

"A hunch that this may turn out to be an interesting day," I answered. "Anything I need to know about?"

"Nothing so far. Somebody threatened a clerk at the 7-Eleven this morning, but it's the one inside the city limits so it's not our problem."

"Where's Jarvis?"

"Since it was so quiet he went to serve those two domestic warrants," Ruby said. "By the way, I was thinking of buying Jarvis something to celebrate him being the new sheriff. Any ideas?"

"How about a six-pack of antacids and aspirin?"

"I don't doubt he'll need them," Ruby said, not returning my smile. "It's a hard job and I've watched it take a lot out of you. Sometimes I think too much. I've prayed about it at times, Sheriff. I pray it hasn't."

I'd worked with Ruby for nine years and it was the first time she'd ever said something so personal to me. I almost smiled and asked if they were Baptist or Catholic prayers, but I caught myself. Why diminish a gift you might have never known you'd been given?

"Thank you, Ruby," I said.

I went into my office and watched the clock's minute hand begin its slow crawl to the top. The warden or his assistant would be at the prison by eight, but eight eastern standard time or central? Knoxville was eastern but Nashville was central. I did a quick Google search and saw Roan Mountain was in the eastern time zone. I set my cell phone on the desk and called Becky on my landline, but same as last night, there was no answer. I checked and there was no e-mail from her. You've got enough to focus on, I reminded myself, but I was worried.

The courthouse clock chimed eight and ten minutes later my cell phone buzzed.

"We'll have it set up for nine o'clock," Joseph said. "We'll call your landline."

I had fifty minutes to kill so I told Ruby I was going over to Greene's Café. I sat alone in my usual booth and studied the list of questions I'd written last night for Carlson. As I sipped my coffee, I thought of a couple more and wrote them down, then folded the paper and stuck it in my shirt pocket. When Lloyd asked if I wanted a refill, I didn't look up, just shook my head.

"You look like you're trying to solve all the world's problems, Sheriff."

"No," I answered, raising my eyes, "just one."

"Well," Lloyd said. "I guess that's a start."

I walked back to the courthouse. Ruby was on the phone but she motioned for me to wait as she said a quick good-bye and hung up.

"I've been meaning to ask you," Ruby said. "What kind of cake would you like at your retirement party, carrot or chocolate. Margie West gets booked up quick, so I was going to get the order in."

"Chocolate," I said and went on to my office.

I'd just sat down when suddenly it was as if I'd stepped off a porch not knowing an abyss lay below. Falling with no rope or steel cable to pull me out. Because retiring hadn't been quite real until this moment. I was fifty-one. My father had lived to seventy-three and he'd been a smoker. What could I expect, thirty years, maybe more? All those hours to fill, and with what? Even if I took the night watchman job, that was part-time. I'd do some farming, and do it organic, but still, come winter, I'd have idle time. Painting, reading . . . what else?

This is what everyone feels when they get ready to retire, I reassured myself. It's a change, and any kind of change can be scary, because you don't have your footing. But then I thought about what I wouldn't be doing—no more visits to inform good people such as Ben Lindsey of a disaster that had befallen someone they loved. I'd never have to walk into a meth house where some child was breathing poison. No, occasional boredom would be fine.

At nine o'clock sharp my landline rang.

"I've got it ready," Joseph said. "I'm hooking you up right now."

"You know what this is about?" I asked once Levon Carlson was on.

"No," Carlson answered, "but I ain't got nothing to say unless you promise me a shorter sentence, or at least a carton of cigarettes."

"Sure," I said. "Just tell me where your cell phone is."

A squawk came from the line's other end.

"That damn bitch I had living with me has it. She wouldn't go my bail but didn't mind gabbing off a thousand minutes on a phone I paid for, then using my credit card number to put more minutes on it."

"All of this was while you were in prison?"

"Hell, yeah," Carlson said, loud enough that I had to hold the receiver farther from my ear. "Them Visa mush heads sent the bill *here*, care of Roan Mountain Correctional Complex, like they figured I was sitting around chewing the fat for hours on a cell phone in a goddamn fucking *prison*. She probably charged panties and Kotex on that card too. They didn't think that a goddamn bit strange either. Damn that bitch and Visa both."

"What's the girl's name?"

"It's Bitch, I'm telling you. First name, middle name, and last."

"Besides that?"

"Besides Bitch?" Carlson said. "She don't deserve no other name."

"I don't care if she deserves it or not. Just calm down and tell me what it is."

"Shiloh," Carlson said, spitting out the word.

"That's her first name?"

"It's a nickname she got from some sappy song."

"Do you know her first or last name?"

"What the hell did I need to know her last name for?" Carlson said indignantly. "I wasn't going to marry her or anything. I was just letting her stay with me awhile. She was probably living under a bridge before that. You'd think she'd be the least bit grateful, but hell no."

"How did you meet her?"

"I used to do some business where I-40 runs over the river. She bought from me there a couple of times. I don't know where she lived, but like I said, I'd not doubt under that bridge."

"Where is she now?"

"I hope in hell, if they'll have her," Carlson said. "But if she's alive, I don't know, unless she's back down there near the interstate."

"How about giving me a description."

"A skank."

"What kind of skank?" I asked. "Blond or brunette, tall, short, fat, skinny? White, black, Latino?"

"Hell, man, white, I got standards. Brown hair. Average height, say five-six, not skinny but not fat either."

"How old?"

"I don't know. I mean she was legal but it wasn't like she was someone's granny."

"That's not giving me a lot as far as a description."

"She's got a tattoo of a rose on her ass," Carlson said.

"You know any of her friends?"

"Mister, she didn't have no friends," Carlson said. "Whatever you're after her about, I hope it's something that puts her in the electric chair. You need a volunteer to pull that switch, I'm your man."

"How about her family?"

"She never said a word about her family."

"And you can't remember her real first and last name?"

"If I could, I'd tell you," Carlson said, "but I never heard her called any name but Shiloh."

"Anything else you can tell me about her?"

"She had lousy taste in music and wouldn't watch anything on TV but game shows and them big-haired preachers," Carlson said, "once in a while a ball game."

"If you think of something else, have Joseph call me."

"So what you going to do for me after all I give you?"

"Unless you come up with something else," I said, "you'll have to settle for a carton of cigarettes."

"Camels," Carlson said.

I thanked Joseph for his help and hung up.

*Shiloh.*

I remembered the song vaguely, something about a boy and girl playing together. In the Bible Shiloh meant *place of peace,* or at least that's what Preacher Waldrop had said in a sermon. He'd claimed you could hear the peacefulness in the word itself. *Shiloh.*

I sat for a few more minutes, thinking about what Carlson had told me, trying to connect it to the fish kill. I called the resort just on the off chance and said I needed to get in touch with a worker named Shiloh. The receptionist said no Shiloh had ever worked there as far as she knew. The next logical call was the Knox County sheriff's office. If she hung out with the likes of Carlson, she'd probably been picked up for something, drugs or prostitution most likely. But then what? Find out she was drugged up and dialed the wrong number, which again seemed about as likely as anything else, or that she'd given the phone to another person, or simply lost it. Carlson, of course, could be lying about the phone, but that was hard to imagine from the way he'd reacted.

I called Knox County and told them what I wanted. They said they'd check their database. It didn't take long. No one with that name, the woman who called back said. I dialed Gerald's number to see if he recognized the name, but no one answered. He was probably out in his garden, or simply too ornery to pick up.

I went to the window. Two boys with baseball gloves walked toward the park. At the intersection a young mother with a stroller waited for the light to change. A blue pickup approached as green switched to yellow, passing beneath the light as it turned red. At least a warning ticket, I thought, since the woman and baby were there.

Then something else, something about the cell phone, stirred in the back of my mind, just as quickly darted back inside. I tried to coax what it was out into the open, but it wouldn't come.

Over the years I'd learned that sometimes the best way to solve a problem was to let it believe you were busy with something else, replacing a burned-out porch light, fixing a leaky faucet. The solution would edge on out and you'd see it clear. I set a trash can beside the desk, on it two clear-plastic trays.

In ten minutes, the drawers were empty. I carried a tray filled with rubber bands and paper clips and pens out to Ruby. The trash can was full but there was little in the other tray. A pocketknife my grandfather had given me, a striped tie, a few dollars' worth of change, an unopened box of watercolor brushes. I could tuck my watercolor and the Hopper painting under my arm and make one trip to the truck instead of two, so I walked over to Hopper's painting to lift it off the hook. But before I did, I studied it a few moments, especially how the red of the freight car contrasted with the yellow of the brush and grass behind it. Yellow and red. Mix them and . . .

# Thirty-two

*Imprismed.* Morning's fawnlight yokes inside dew beads, each hued like a rainbow's hatchling. But they cling like tears about to fall. Memory cascades, last night with Gerald, the drawn gun at the resort, Richard, all rushing toward the cliffs of fall, the fall of footsteps. I roll up my sleeping bag and ride past the park entrance and the resort. I leave the bike and enter the woods. But not to Gerald's house. I enter his barn and climb into the loft. I lie on the straw and I can't hold it back and it all comes again . . .

*Promise me, children, not a single word,* Ms. Abernathy had whispered. Then she'd led us down the hallway single file to the basement doorway, into the cave feeling of tight walls and cool dark. I am the very last, reaching for Ms. Abernathy's hand as we make our way to the basement's concrete floor. There we are, long moments silent, the only sound pipedrip. Light slants pale yellow on the stairs we came down. Dust motes drift within, as if to say *No one's passed through here in years*. No other light but what leaks from the other basement door Ms. Abernathy herds us toward. Almost there when her *shhhhh* stills us. Footsteps come halfway down the basement stairs and pause. Both my hands clutch Ms. Abernathy's. Another footstep and a shoe and a pants cuff appear. The pipe drips loud and my first tears well. I try to squeeze them back inside me but the first one splats on the concrete floor and I know he has heard it, and I look up to tell Ms. Abernathy and she covers my mouth with her hand but too late and the paused feet come down the stairs.

## Thirty-three

The number was still on my desk pad and I dialed it. Joseph wasn't in, but when I told the new guard what I wanted he said he'd go ask.

"Carlson said blue."

I called Jarvis's cell phone.

"I need you to go get Darby Ramsey. Don't give him a reason. There's probably a woman out there with him but don't bother with her. Just bring Darby in. You got all that?"

"Yes," Jarvis said.

"There's one other thing. Once you're on the way back, ask him how Shiloh's doing."

"Shiloh?"

"Yeah, just ask how she's doing. Then call me if he acts

like he knows who you're talking about. Just say 'affirmative,' if you call."

"Nothing else?" Jarvis said.

"Nothing else."

You could still be wrong, I reminded myself, but I didn't believe that. No, it was Darby. What I didn't know was *why*. It would take Jarvis fifteen minutes to get to Darby's house. I tried to turn my thoughts to how nice it would be next summer sitting on my cabin porch, but my eyes kept drifting back to the black office phone.

It finally rang.

"Affirmative," Jarvis said.

"Did you see her as well?"

"Affirmative."

"Bring Darby on in," I said, "and keep him in the office until I get back."

I put on my gun and holster and left. I wasn't trying to drive fast but the speedometer kept lifting. In a few minutes I passed Jarvis coming the other way, Darby in the backseat. When I turned onto Otter Creek Road, I thought about setting the blue light on my dash to shake her up, but decided something other than drugs might go down the toilet. If the phone was still around.

I slowed when the barn came in sight, then pulled off in front of the farmhouse. She wasn't on the porch. I didn't knock, just turned the knob and opened the door. She was in a recliner, watching a game show turned up too loud. She wore jeans like last time, but instead of the orange University of Tennessee football jersey, a man's flannel shirt covered her wasted frame. How much weight had she lost since Levon Carlson had last seen her? At least thirty pounds. On a stool beside the chair was a bag of blue crystals and a glass pipe. I stepped all the way in and she finally noticed me. An orange Bic lighter was in her hand. She closed her palm over it, as if concealing the lighter might make the drugs and pipe disappear too.

I picked up the remote and turned off the television.

"You're not waiting until Darby gets back, Shiloh?" I asked. "That's smart on your part, because he's in some serious trouble. I'm just hoping he hasn't gotten you in it too."

She looked at me and whatever she felt was not surprise, which said as much about her life as anything. Nights spent under bridges, sordid acts done for drugs, beatings, rapes, she lived in a world where bad things never strayed for long. Robin Lindsey in another year or two, I couldn't help thinking, if Robin wasn't in jail or dead.

"You've got Levon Carlson's cell phone and I need it," I told her, raising an open palm when she started to deny it. "Don't speak, just listen. Give me the cell phone and answer a couple of questions and I'll walk out of here. I'll even leave your baggie and your pipe. But if you don't tell me where the phone is, I'm going to take you straight to jail. So what's it going to be?"

"Darby will kill me if I tell you," she answered.

"No, he won't. I know you called his uncle, and I know that was Darby's idea, not yours, same as I figure somebody else was in on it besides you two."

"You ain't going to arrest me having that?" she asked, nodding at the baggie.

"Not today, Shiloh. You get a free pass on everything, if you answer my questions."

"You swear," she said, more doubt than hope in her voice.

"Yes."

She looked at the pipe and baggie, then back at me.

"All I done was tell that old man he needed to meet someone at a waterfall."

"That's a start, but where's the cell phone?"

"You're not trying to trick me," she said, "by saying you won't charge me today but charging me tomorrow?"

"No."

Shiloh still didn't look like she quite believed me, but let out a sigh and laid the lighter on the stool.

"I sold it."

"Who'd you sell it to?"

"That pawnshop outside town, the one near CVS," Shiloh said. "Darby told me to throw it in the river but I knew I could get some cash for it. It was got rid of, that was the important thing."

"Who else helped Darby do this?"

"I don't know. He wouldn't tell me."

"Nobody came here to talk to him?"

"Well, one night someone drove up," Shiloh said. "Darby told me to stay inside, so I didn't see him. After that, Darby talked to whoever it was, but it was always over the phone."

"Your cell phone or a different one?" I asked.

"Mine."

"You remember the last time they talked?"

"Is today Friday?"

"Yes."

She counted back on her fingers.

"I'm pretty sure it was Tuesday."

"Okay," I said, "but if that cell phone's not at the pawnshop, I'm coming back."

"I took it on Wednesday. The man in there, he'll tell you so. It's blue and has a chipped place on the corner. If he sold it, that's not my fault."

I took a pen from my pocket.

"I'll need your password."

"S H I L O 18."

I wrote the password on a piece of paper and tucked it in my shirt pocket.

"Is that how you spell your name?"

"Except for the numbers."

"But it's not your real name?"

"No," she answered. "But if I get a free pass like you claim, I don't figure you need the real one."

"Fair enough," I said.

She looked ready to say something else but hesitated.

"What?" I asked.

"None of this would have happened if Darby had been given what was his by right."

"Which was?"

"That old man's land," Shilo said. "It's done promised to Darby but the old fool won't give it over."

"What's Darby wanting it for?"

"Him and that other fellow was going to sell it."

"To the resort?"

"He didn't tell me who to," Shilo answered. "Darby just said if that old man had sold the land a few years ago, it'd have brought a bunch more money and Darby wouldn't have had to share a dime of it."

"So Darby thought if his uncle got arrested, he'd get the land?"

"I don't know. Darby just said that him and the other fellow had things figured out and I didn't need to know anything else about it."

Because Trey kept later hours on Friday, he wouldn't

be at his pawnshop yet, so I called his house. I asked about the blue phone and he said he still had it. It's important, I told him. Trey said he'd meet me at his shop.

"I told you he had it," Shilo said.

Darby's truck was parked outside, so I gave it a quick look. A five-gallon can was in the bed, a price sticker still on it. I lifted the can and smelled not kerosene but gas.

# Thirty-four

"Becky?" Then after a few more moments, my name called again. I shift my body to peek between the board slats. A piece of straw drifts down, then another. Gerald steps farther into the barn and stands beside the loft ladder. He has two cups of coffee in his hands.

"I saw you come in here a few minutes ago," he says, looking up as he speaks. "Last night, the way I acted. To treat you that way, after all you done for me. It was wrong. I'm sorry."

For a few moments the barn is completely still.

"Anyway, I brought you some coffee. I'll leave it here by the ladder if it's your rather, but you could sit on the porch with me and drink it. That's what I'd like, you sitting with me on the porch."

I wait a few more moments, then slowly get up. I wipe the straw off my shirt and pants and climb down.

"I made it fresh," Gerald says, and hands me a cup.

A barn swallow swoops in, dips low, then lifts. The chevroned wings fold and it settles in the nest. Gerald stares at a tangle of tools—shovel and hoes, sickles and pitchforks. Some lean but most are long fallen, metal and helve imprinting the straw.

"This barn's some mess, ain't it?" Gerald says.

"I'd be glad to help you clean it up."

Gerald shakes his head.

"No reason to," he says softly.

We walk out of the barn. Gerald moves slow and holds the handrail as he steps up to the porch.

"Are you all right?" I ask as we sit down. "Do you need your pills?"

Gerald shakes his head and for a few minutes we look out at the mountains and sip our coffee.

"Those speckled trout we saw in the pool," Gerald says when he sets his cup beside the chair, "that kerosene didn't kill them, did it?"

"No, they're fine."

"Good," Gerald says. "There's something I need you to do for me, okay?"

"Of course. What is it?"

"I got it in my will to have that cremation done to me.

Agnes said it goes against the Bible, that you're supposed to wait for the resurrection whole and in the ground proper buried. But the part of William that come back from the war, it wouldn't fill an apple crate. If God's got a mind to hold that against William, then he'll have to hold it against me too. I've got plenty to account for in my life, but if that one tips the scales against me, so be it. What I'm asking Becky, it ain't in the will. Those ashes, spread them on Agnes's and William's graves, but keep a handful to put by the pool where them speckled trout are. Right there on the sand. You'll do that for me, won't you?"

The phone inside rings but Gerald doesn't get up, motions for me not to either. Then my cell phone buzzes and it's Les. I walk into the yard and answer. Les asks if I'm with Gerald and I say yes.

"I found out who made the call," Les tells me, "and she admitted it."

Moments pass but I don't speak.

"Are you there?" Les asks.

I manage a soft yes.

"I've still got a couple of things I don't understand, but I wanted you to know there was a call."

"It proves Gerald didn't do this, doesn't it?"

"Not quite," Les says, "but I'll know more soon."

I go back on the porch and tell Gerald but he doesn't say anything.

"Don't you understand, Gerald?" I tell him. "This is all but over. People will know the truth. Everyone, not just Les and me."

"That is good," Gerald finally says. "But I'm tired, Becky, too tired to care anymore."

"Of course you're tired," I say. "Anyone would be after what you've been through. But you can rest up this weekend and you'll be fine."

"Maybe so," Gerald says.

"We've got lots more things to do, starting with getting that garden harvested and cutting more wood for the winter. You're not going to make me do all that by myself, are you? You know I'm no good with a chain saw. I'd probably cut my arm off."

For the first time, Gerald smiles. It's a weary smile, but it's real.

"I'd be a sorry sort of fellow to let that happen."

"You would," I say, and nod at his cup. "I'll go in and get us a refill."

"Sounds good," Gerald says, but as I take the cup from his hand, he holds on to it. "But what I asked you to do, you'll do it?"

"Yes."

# *Thirty-five*

Trey was waiting in his truck when I turned in. He unlocked the door and I was about to follow him when he stopped me.

"You better wait here a minute, hoss," Trey said, opening the door wider so more light came in. A piece of what looked like kite string was tied to the inside doorknob. The other end crossed the floor to a round shape beside the display case. As my eyes adjusted to the dimness, the coiled body, triangle head, and pale rattles emerged.

"You thought I was bullshitting about that fellow being out, didn't you?" Trey said as he crossed the room, giving the snake a wide berth as he retrieved the phone.

"This one?" Trey asked, handing me the blue cell phone and the charger wrapped around it.

"Yes," I said, my thumb finding the chipped corner.

I looked at the rattlesnake, which had not moved since we'd come in. The string was knotted to the neck ring.

"How do you get it back in the aquarium?"

"Oh, that's an easy thing," Trey said. "Just pin his head with my snake stick, undo the slipknot, and grab him behind the neck. Getting him out is the devil of it."

"Mind if I hold on to this phone a day or two? If we need to keep it, I'll make out a requisition form."

"Don't bother," he said. "I only paid seven dollars. Think of it as a retirement present."

Trey followed me outside.

"Ben Lindsey came in yesterday afternoon," Trey said.

"To check if anything Robin took had shown up?"

"No, to sell his high school ring. He took it off right in front of me and laid it on the counter. He kept his finger on it a few moments, like we were playing checkers, then pushed it toward me. I don't usually notice things like that, or at least try not to. Ben said he'd be bringing some other things soon." Trey shook his head and grimaced, then set his hand on the doorknob. "I did give him more than a fair price for that ring, but I still felt like shit taking it."

Trey went inside and I drove on to the courthouse, parked but didn't get out. I figured I'd have to charge the phone first but I pressed the power button and it lit up. I tapped in the password and checked the recent calls. Numbers lined up smooth as slots. The last number was Gerald's, the one before and after it the same number, an 828 area code. But not the resort's number.

"Charlotte called right after you left," Ruby said when I entered the main office. "They had a body at the morgue they thought might be Robin Lindsey, but they just called back and it's not."

Ruby shook her head.

"I don't think Ben Lindsey could have stood it if it had been. The way that man looked when he came in here on Tuesday."

"I know," I said and went into my office where Darby sulked like a schoolkid waiting for the principal. Jarvis was in my chair, reading a *Field & Stream*. Jarvis started to get up but I motioned for him to stay.

"You got no right doing me like this," Darby said. "He ain't even told me why I'm here."

I took the cell phone out of my pocket and Darby's face went slack.

"Your Rocky Top girl sold it to Trey Yarbrough for seven dollars," I said. "That was smart of her, don't you think, instead of throwing a perfectly good phone in the river? She also told me you had her call Gerald."

"I don't know nothing about any of that," Darby said.

I stared at him for a few moments. In little more than

a month, the meth had whittled him down considerably. Eye sockets more hollow, jaw and cheekbones sharper. Even his greasy hair. It now swept winglike over his ears, bringing to mind skulls carved on old gravestones or sewn on biker jackets.

"You can't inherit Gerald's money for any reason other than death. You were told that but I guess you're so drugged up you forgot." I turned to Jarvis. "You guess that's it?"

"Heck," Jarvis said, knowing what I was up to. "He doesn't even know what the word *inherit* means."

"I know he's got to be dead first," Darby sneered.

"Then why did you do it?" I asked.

"I ain't saying another word till I'm lawyered up."

I nodded at the blue cell phone.

"The calls and numbers are in there, including one that came in at 8:10 on Tuesday night. I'm going to find out who that number belongs to. Even if the other phone *is* in the river, I've got the number and I know someone who can track it down real quick. So here's the thing, Darby. You can tell me whose number this is and what all of this is about and be the one who the judge knows cooperated, or you can let your partner play that card."

I tapped the power switch on and read the number out loud.

"I'm going to press CALL in one minute, Darby, and if

I do I'm picking up every rain check and IOU I've got with the prosecutor's office. They may put you in Guantanamo before I'm finished."

Darby rubbed a hand over his forehead, like he was trying to summon a genie, or at least a good lie. A fingernail and thumbnail clicked against each other on his free hand. He gave a slight nod, then clenched both hands in his lap and met my eyes.

"I done it so the old bastard would hurry up and die," Darby said.

I looked at Jarvis, who shrugged his shoulders.

"I don't understand."

"You ought to," Darby said, giving me a weak smile. "It was partly your idea, Sheriff."

The chair squeaked as Jarvis got up.

"I'm going to get a cup of coffee," he said. "I'll be back in twenty."

"I ain't claiming your boss is in on it," Darby said, but Jarvis walked on out and shut the door behind him.

"What are you getting at?" I asked.

"What you told C.J. Gant about old folks like Gerald, how they don't last long once you get them out of their house and in a new place. He said you were right about that, so C.J. figured if the arrest and trial didn't kill a man who'd had two heart attacks, then for sure jail or a nuthouse would."

"C.J. Gant?" I said. "The same one who worked at the resort?"

"The one and only."

"You're lying," I said. "You're only saying that because Tucker fired him. Don't you dare try to drag C.J. into this."

"Drag him into it," Darby snorted. "He come to me, not me to him. It was all his idea. I was fucking *coerced*, ain't that the word for it? He came the other night to my house. Of course he stayed out in his car, like he was too good to come in. Asked me how I'd like to get my inheritance in eight months tops, and a decent price for the property to boot."

"This is really about Tucker wanting to get that land, not C.J., isn't it?"

"Hell no," Darby said. "Tucker don't want that land. Dumbass Gerald let that gravy train roll on down the line two years ago. C.J. said he'd help me get at least half a million. Claimed folks still wanted to buy land up here but you had to know how to find them."

For a few moments I didn't speak. Everything was off-plumb. It was like a movie where the dialogue's out of sync, a movie I was in, though I damn well wished I wasn't, because, slowly, what seemed out of sync became less and less so.

"Why?"

"Why what?" Darby asked.

"Why would C.J. help you?"

"Why?" Darby said, looking at me incredulously. "Goddamn thirty percent is why. He's a crafty son of a bitch. He told me Gerald could live ten more years easy, just out of pure stubbornness. He's right too. It'd be just like Uncle Gerald to keep himself alive to spite me. So I asked what if his plan didn't work. If he ain't dead in eight months, you don't owe me a dime, he told me. Made it like a bet. Of course, I ended up doing all the real work, like lugging that kerosene up there. All he done was tell me where the resort's cameras were. If I knew I could sell that land on my own, and quick, the way C.J. claimed he could, I'd have said the hell with him."

Darby bit his lower lip, cursed softly.

"We should have done what I said."

"What was that?"

"Burn Gerald's house down. Matter of fact, I was all for doing that first but C.J. said this was safer, no arson investigators, or risk of being spotted at Gerald's place."

"You'd have done it with Gerald in the house?"

"No need for that," Darby said. "We'd have waited while he was off to town or church, made it look like it started in the fireplace. Like I told C.J., soon as Gerald saw it he'd have keeled over right then and there. He'd figure God or something was getting back at him for burning William's house down. But even if that didn't do it, he wouldn't be living in that farmhouse no more. If the fish kill didn't work, that was what we were going to do next. It would have been the sure thing to put him in the ground." Darby shook his head and sighed. "If we'd have done it that way, we'd already have a FOR SALE sign in the ground."

# Thirty-six

---

A snapping turtle hauls itself toward the stream. Not a short journey: the shell's gray mosaic dusted brown. To this meadow from where? A smaller stream? Or some miles off, a drought-drained pond? I think of my grandfather in another meadow years ago, a divining rod trembling in his hand. *Right here,* he'd told his neighbor. I'd been with him that day, but had there really been water? If I was told, I have no memory of it.

Soon Gerald and I will be on his porch stringing beans and filling a washtub. We'll ponder the mountains, watch the woolly worm's coat to see how cold the winter will be. Watch fog saddle the mountainsides white. Soon.

I look at what I've written and watch the turtle move

through the grass, over the spoon dip of the trail, into woods soon slanting toward water.

> From the dying drool of a farm pond
> where deep-most dock legs are dry,
> let it plod through field and pasture
> to find lasting water, let it pulse
> the creek pool's muddy heart,
> then rise, a slow becoming,
> like a bruise summoning
> its own harsh beauty
> and survive

If not today then soon, gray clouds will gather. Let it come so I might hear leaf splats, watch the wet blotch, taste on my tongue, feel on my face the pentecost of petrichor. And afterward:

> as the storm moves on
> rain trickles off
> the leaves
> like an afterthought

# *Thirty-seven*

When Jarvis came back, I had him take Darby downstairs and put him in a cell. No paperwork yet, I said. I told Ruby I needed to be left alone and shut my door. After twenty minutes I'd thought and rethought things enough to make a choice. I spent the next hour making phone calls and typing up a confession, then told Jarvis to bring Darby back upstairs.

I pointed at a seat and closed the door. Darby set his left leg over his right knee, then began scratching his ankle. Thinking of that bag of crystal Shilo was dipping into at that very moment. Or at least his body was thinking about it. But then I saw it wasn't meth bugs. Darby's sock had a hole and his fingers tugged at the cloth to conceal it. Sent to prison twice for theft, then trying to kill his own uncle, but a worn-out sock was what shamed him.

"Here's the deal," I said, pushing paper and pen to his side of the desk.

"You're crazy as a shit-house rat if you figure me to sign that," Darby said after reading it.

"You'll sign it," I said, "because if you don't all kinds of bad things are going to happen to you."

"Like what?"

"I'll go back over to your house and get the drugs your lady friend showed me. Third offense is another year in prison guaranteed, added on to what you'll get for the fish kill."

"They'll lock me up longer if I take all the blame for it," Darby said.

"I talked to the DA and to Tucker too. I said I could get the guilty person to turn himself in for a bit of leniency. The DA's willing to let you off with a five-thousand-dollar fine, no jail time. Tucker wasn't a damn bit happy, but he said if he got ten thousand in restitution he'd accept the deal."

"I ain't got that kind of money," Darby said.

"I'm paying it," I said, "the fine and Tucker both."

Darby cocked his head and stared at me. It was the look of a man who wouldn't trust his own shadow.

"There's another thing for you to think about," I said. "You were right about Becky Shytle wanting your inheritance, but she wants it for the park, not herself. I helped her figure out how to do it too. The short of it is, Gerald will donate the land to the state."

"Bullshit," Darby said.

"You think so," I said. "I can't imagine why Gerald wouldn't go along with it, can you, especially after you tried to put him in jail?"

"He promised Momma . . ."

I smiled.

"That's why the donation will be in *your* name, Darby, not Gerald's. It will be *your* land that's been donated, and don't you worry, you'll get all the credit for it. There'll be a plaque at the park with 'Donated by Darby Ramsey' engraved on it. They're nice plaques, Darby, not some cheap thing like you'd get at Walmart. It even has a gold finish, and Becky will make sure they put it where everyone can see your name."

"This ain't near right," Darby said, and said it again, this time more a moan than a statement. He stared at the paper and then settled two fingers on the ink pen but didn't pick it up.

"So what's your pleasure, Darby?"

"What else have I got to do?" Darby asked. "That is, if I sign it?"

"Nothing else, except that, once you do sign it, you understand that dragging C.J. Gant into this will do you no good. Who will believe you if it's your word against a guy who built a park for kids? And this cell phone, it's going to disappear too. You'll have nothing to link it to him but your word. But even so, if you do mention C.J. was involved in this, *ever*, I'll kick your ass so hard you'll be shitting out of your ears."

"What about Shilo?"

"She's not going to be brought up in any of this, same as C.J. And if you do anything to her for talking to me, I'll kick your ass for that too."

"So I take all the blame."

"Sign that paper and you're every bit as free as them."

Darby stared at the window, no doubt wishing he was somewhere other than here.

"So I'll just walk out soon as I sign it. No bond or anything?"

"That's right."

"How do I know you won't go back on your word after I sign this," Darby asked, "and me end up in prison anyway?"

"I won't do that."

"Why not?"

There were a couple of answers I could give, but I picked the one Darby would believe.

"Maybe it's because I think you'll die quicker outside of prison than in."

For the first time since we'd sat down, Darby met

my eyes. The mask of bravado and swagger drained away. What was left wasn't hopefulness or hopelessness, sadness or happiness, relief or fear. I couldn't put a name to it, but I knew it was human, and then it drained away as well.

"Okay," Darby muttered. "I'll sign it."

I brought Ruby in as a witness and Darby signed the confession. As soon as he left I took out the blue cell phone and dialed the number. C.J. picked up on the third ring.

"We need to talk, C.J.," I said. "I'll meet you at the park in twenty minutes."

He still didn't speak.

"I've already talked to Darby."

"All right," he said.

I drove to my house and got the money I'd hidden in the attic. Sat at the kitchen table and I counted out the fifteen thousand for the fine and restitution and then another twenty-five thousand to pay for the porch. After all the ugliness I'd seen as a sheriff, I figured I was at least owed a pretty view. I put the eighty-five thousand in a paper shopping bag and drove back. I parked at the courthouse and walked down to the park. The air was less humid, cleaner feeling, and the blue sky had the clarity you get this time of year. People were out, getting an early start to their weekend. As I sat down on a bench, I saw Barry and his family. Carly stood under a tree near the swing set, the baby in the bassinet beside her, while Delila, their three-year-old, caught a ball Barry tossed underhanded. I walked a few yards toward them and waved. Barry opened a palm in response but turned back to his daughter.

I would have gone and spoken if Barry had looked my way again, but he didn't, so I sat back down and closed my eyes, leaned my head upward to feel the sun's warmth. When Sarah and I went to Laurel Fork that afternoon, I'd asked her to marry me. Then we'd skinny-dipped in a pool below a waterfall. The water was icy cold but we hadn't toweled off or wrapped ourselves in the quilt we'd brought. We just lay on a big slab of rock near the tailrace. Side by side, silent, just one of my hands touching one of hers as the sun warmed us. After a few minutes, we'd gotten up. Sarah nodded at where our bodies had made damp shadows. *You know there will be times I'll be like that,* she'd said, pointing at her shadow. *Sometimes the pills aren't enough. There may be times you'll wish . . . No I won't,* I'd said and pulled her to me. *There will never be a single moment I'll think anything but how lucky I am to have you as my wife. I promise.* Then we'd made love. Afterward, Sarah had gone back into the water. I stood on the bank and watched her swim to the pool's center, disappear, and resurface, her throat lifting as she swept back her hair with one hand, her eyes meeting mine as she waded back to shore unclothed, her hair and skin glistening, her bare feet stepping softly over the river rocks, coming closer with her damp arms already open to embrace me. She'd pressed her head against my heart. Promise me again, Sarah had said. *I promise*, I'd said.

I opened my eyes and watched Barry and his family. I hoped that he no longer awakened in the night to drag a vacuum cleaner across a floor, straighten a towel, or wipe off a counter. I imagined him waking at 2 or 3 A.M. and realizing *I don't need to do that anymore*, then placing an arm around Carly's waist, closing the space between them.

I looked around the park C.J. had made possible, thought back to that afternoon when C.J. had saved my arm, surely my life. I wanted to believe I'd have done the same for him, but I knew that I would have hesitated, if just for a second, and it would have been too late.

C.J. drove up, not in his SUV but a Ford Escort I'd seen on Bob Ponder's used car lot. He came and sat down, looking out at the park, as I did.

"So you had the camera connected to your office computer?" I asked.

"Yes."

A child got on the swing set, and her father pushed to get her going. She rose and fell, legs straight out, hands gripping the chains. At the top of the arc, she squeezed the chains tight and lifted a few inches out of the swing, for a moment airborne and weightless.

After a couple of minutes, C.J. spoke.

"If you expect me to say I'm sorry I did it, that's not

going to happen. I stuck my neck out for Gerald and you see what he did to me, what he did to my boys' futures. You know with that bad heart he won't live much longer. Then Darby will sell the land and spend every penny on drugs. You tell me that won't happen? The one chance that money could do some good was helping my boys. Tell me that's not true?"

"Even if it is all true . . . ," I said, and for a moment it was like I'd lost my train of thought.

"Even if it is all true *what?*"

"It was still wrong, C.J."

"Okay, it was wrong. Is that what you need to hear, me saying it myself?"

"I just couldn't expect you to do this," I answered.

My words sounded convoluted, even to me.

"You know I didn't want to come back up here," C.J. said, not looking at me or the girl swinging but at the mountains. "Another head of PR job was opening soon at Myrtle Beach. Same raise in pay as here. I told Mr. Tucker the Myrtle Beach job was the one I wanted, but because of the expansions, he needed me here for the politics since, like him, I *understood* the local culture. A year, at most two, he told me, and I'd be back at Myrtle Beach, with a big promotion and a bump in salary. So I came back, because it was the best thing I could do for my boys. Then the recession hits and I'm stuck in the same county I spent my early life trying to get out of. But even so, once I got here, I tried to do some good. I told myself that this was where I came from, that despite everything, this was *home* and I could make it a better place. And not just for me. I've done a lot of good for this community, more than I had to for the job. I spent *my* time, not Tucker's, to get this park and the new fire station built. And now, people in this town, the same ones who looked down on me growing up, they're glad I got fired. So fuck Gerald and fuck this whole town."

C.J. paused.

"Go ahead," he said, "tell me how that dumbass couldn't even get rid of a six-ounce cell phone."

"His girlfriend sold it to Trey Yarbrough, for seven dollars."

C.J. shook his head.

"And they say you can't go home again, right, Les? Well, I'm back and nothing's changed. The same people doing the same stupid things. *My people.* Who've never done a damn thing for me. The only college scholarship money I got from this county came from the Knights of Columbus, folks who had moved here from other places. Yeah, my people, who resented me when I treated them the same way they'd treated me growing up. You don't think I've heard them? *Why that's old Darnell Gant's boy. Look at him all dressed up. His daddy used to be the biggest drunk in this county, and now he thinks he's some hotshot because he works for Tucker at that resort."*

C.J. turned to me.

"There have been times you did the same. I've seen it at council meetings, heard your little quips."

"Maybe I did some of that, but I've defended you too."

"So what now?" C.J. asked. "Are you arresting me?"

"No, this is over. Darby's signed a confession that he acted alone. That's part of the deal, that he won't bring you into it."

"And you believe he'll keep quiet about me, despite the confession?"

"I know he will. Greed and fear are a potent combination."

"What about the phone?"

I took the blue cell phone out of my pocket and set it between us.

"You want to get rid of it or you want me to?"

C.J. put the phone in his pocket. I nodded toward the Escort.

"Traded cars, I see."

"When you don't have a job, you have to do things like that."

"You'll find another job. Tucker told me he'll give you a good recommendation."

"There's a little more irony," C.J. said, looking out at the park. "The person who's been the most decent to me in this county is the one who fired me."

"Any prospects yet, for jobs I mean."

"If I'm completely off the hook, as you say, I've a good chance at a job in Florida."

"You are."

"I'm going for an interview next week. Tucker actually called the CEO, told him about me. Of course, it pays half of what I made here. Jane will have to find a new job too, and in this economy, we'll lose all sorts of money on our house. The boys' college money will be down to near nothing, maybe tuition for a year at a state school."

"You'll give them more than your parents gave you," I said. "You already have."

"And how hard is that, Les?" C.J. said, turning to me. "Sending them off with a comb and toothbrush would be more than what I got."

Across the park, Barry and his family were leaving, Carly and the baby already heading to the car. Barry looked my way and I waved. He waved as well, then kneeled to lift his daughter. Her arms locked around his neck as he rose and walked toward the car.

"Darby told me that you two thought about burning Gerald's house down."

C.J. shrugged.

"I don't believe you would have done that. Darby would do it, but not you."

"Believe what you want," C.J. said, and paused. "I suppose I should ask why you're letting this end here instead of court."

"Let's just say my last couple of weeks will be easier if it does."

"If I get that Florida job," C.J. said, pressing his hands against his knees to rise, "I'll never come back here, not even for a day."

"Take this with you," I said, and set the paper bag between us.

"What is it?"

I opened the bag so he could see.

"Scholarship money for your boys from the County Hemp Growers Association."

C.J. looked around.

"Is somebody filming this?"

"I hope not."

C.J. left the bag where it was.

"What do you expect me to do, Les? Show you I've got enough self-worth left not to take it? That I've still got enough of that Appalachian *pride* left in me? You could be mistaken. I learned early in life that I'd better look after myself, not other people."

"That's not true of the morning we were working at your uncle's."

"I didn't have time to think about what I was doing."

"You did the same with Gerald in June. Like you said, you turned left instead of right."

"So?"

"I've never had a moment like that," I answered. "My first instinct, my nature, is always what's best for me."

"And you see where my 'nature' has gotten me."

"It got you a family, C.J., sons and a wife who love you. I've seen them with you. It's obvious."

For a few moments we didn't speak.

"This 'scholarship' money," C.J. said. "If I do take it, will your donors know who's receiving it? I'd rather not have them coming to my door sometime wanting it back."

"No one but you and me will know about this."

C.J. cursed softly.

"It's not money for you, C.J., but for your boys and it will help them. Like you said about Gerald's money, it will do some good."

"Damnit," C.J. said, and picked up the bag, setting it on his lap. He crinkled the bag tighter.

"If this is about paying me back for what happened on my uncle's farm that day," C.J. said, "I can write you a note 'Paid in Full.'"

"That's not necessary."

"Anything else on our agenda?"

"No."

"Then I'm leaving," C.J. said, and got up.

I watched him walk back to his car. He didn't thank me, but that seemed only fair.

# Thirty-eight

When I returned to my office, the space seemed transformed although I'd left less than an hour earlier. It had the hollow feel of a house after the moving van departs. I heard it in my footsteps as I walked over to the window and looked out at the town. Jarvis knocked and came in. I told him what had happened. Not everything, but enough.

"Hell of a week," Jarvis said. "If the next two are as bad as this one I may be retiring with you."

"I doubt they will be," I answered, but I knew something would surely happen involving Robin Lindsey, and I'd be making another trip to Ben and Martha's house. There'd likely be another meth bust, a few other calamities.

"What about that National Forest road?" Jarvis asked. "Should we keep checking it?"

"I doubt you'll catch anybody, but an occasional visit might make them think twice about being there."

"Sounds good," Jarvis said. "You want me to go get that ankle monitor off Gerald?"

"No, I'll do it."

Jarvis nodded and went out to the main office.

Since I'd be pretty much emptying my savings account to pay Billy Orr, I called Pat Newton to accept the night watchman job. Then I sat down and thought about some things before going downstairs to get the diagonal cutters for the ankle monitor. I drove past the hospital and soon crossed over the Parkway onto Locust Creek Road. But before I went to Gerald's house, I turned off. I parked and walked onto the bridge. Becky was downstream with a group of children. I waved and then waited until she'd finished and the school bus had pulled out of the lot.

"I knew he was innocent," she says, her voice muffled as she presses her head against my chest, her arms that encircle me tightening more.

"And you were right."

We hold each other awhile longer, saying nothing until a camper pulls into the lot beside us.

"I need to talk to you," I say, taking her hand and crossing over the bridge so we can be alone together.

Paw pads rock-sore and thorned from the long coming forth   climbing out of the world's understory   those cave depths where swervelight leads   past a hand pressed fast to the wall then out of the dark and onto land leveled   making its way through oilfields and highways across the rio grande and then the colorado   in a bayou's dark water passing   under the shadow of the last ivorybill   across flat black belt fields until land rolls and reddens   back into mountains thick-treed and quick-watered   where one stream is found and it alone followed guided upstream by the moon's silver shining   past a tangle of sticks the scat of an otter   and now in this moment the front paw is lowered   in the silence of fast-filling sand   the first words and last words are printed.

*I was here*

## Acknowledgments

Heartfelt thanks to the following for their support and input on this novel: Warren Buckner, Jim Casada, Jill Gottesman, Dan Halpern, Eleanor Kriseman, Megan Lynch, Victoria Mathews, Phil Moore, Kathy Rash, Tom Rash, Michael Radescula, Marly Rusoff, Randall Wilhelm, and Western Carolina University. Most of all thanks to Ann, Caroline, and James.

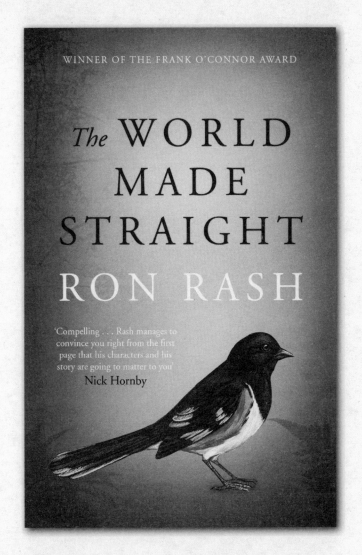

*The* WORLD
MADE
STRAIGHT

RON RASH

'Compelling . . . Rash manages to
convince you right from the first
page that his characters and his
story are going to matter to you'
Nick Hornby

'Exhilarating . . . compelling literature'
*Los Angeles Times*

CANON‖GATE

RON RASH

SERENA

'A bloody – and bloody brilliant – story of passion and revenge . . .
There has never been a heroine quite like this'
*The Times*

'Bitter and brilliant . . . the plot moves with precision,
beautifully wrought' *Guardian*

CANON▌▌GATE

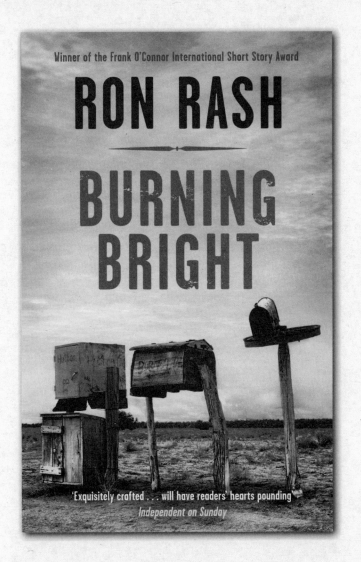

# RON RASH

# BURNING BRIGHT

'Exquisitely crafted . . . will have readers' hearts pounding
*Independent on Sunday*

'Superb; the great American short story at its best'
*The Times*

CANON GATE